MORRIS AUTOMATED INFORMATION NETWORK

0 1029 06821

W9-AUW-191

Parsippany-Troy Hills Library
Main Library
449 Halsey RD
Parsippany NJ 07054
973-887-5150

NOV 0 3 2016

WITHDRAWN

HOW TO AVOID EXTINCTION

HOW TO AVOID EXTINCTION

PAUL ACAMPORA

Scholastic Press | *New York*

Copyright © 2016 by Paul Acampora
Allosaur art by Glendon Mellow

All rights reserved. Published by Scholastic Press, an imprint of Scholastic Inc.,
Publishers since 1920. SCHOLASTIC, SCHOLASTIC PRESS, and associated logos are
trademarks and/or registered trademarks of Scholastic Inc.

The publisher does not have any control over and does not assume any responsibility
for author or third-party websites or their content.

No part of this publication may be reproduced, stored in a retrieval system, or
transmitted in any form or by any means, electronic, mechanical, photocopying,
recording, or otherwise, without written permission of the publisher. For
information regarding permission, write to Scholastic Inc., Attention: Permissions
Department, 557 Broadway, New York, NY 10012.

This book is a work of fiction. Names, characters, places, and incidents are either the
product of the author's imagination or are used fictitiously, and any resemblance to
actual persons, living or dead, business establishments, events, or locales is entirely
coincidental.

Library of Congress Cataloging-in-Publication Data

Names: Acampora, Paul, author.
Title: How to avoid extinction / Paul Acampora.
Description: First edition. | New York : Scholastic Press, 2016. | ©2016 | Summary: Leo's
    grandfather died a year ago, and ever since Leo has been tasked with tracking his
    grandmother down whenever she wanders away from their home in Allentown,
    Pennsylvania—but when she abruptly decides to take the trip to Utah that her husband
    was planning, Leo finds himself on the way to visit dinosaurs, in an old Buick with his
    grandmother, his seventeen-year-old cousin Abby, and Abby's old, smelly Golden
    retriever, Kermit, without telling his mother.
Identifiers: LCCN 2016007973 | ISBN 9780545899062 (hardcover)
Subjects: LCSH: Grandmothers—Juvenile fiction. | Grandparent and child—Juvenile
    fiction. | Voyages and travels—Juvenile fiction. | Families—Juvenile fiction. | Mothers
    and sons—Juvenile fiction. | CYAC: Grandmothers—Fiction. | Grandparent and child—
    Fiction. | Voyages and travels—Fiction. | Automobile travel—Fiction. | Family life—
    Fiction. | Mothers and sons—Fiction.
Classification: LCC PZ7.A17298 Ho 2016 | DDC 813.6—dc23
LC record available at http://lccn.loc.gov/2016007973

10 9 8 7 6 5 4 3 2 1   16 17 18 19 20
Printed in the U.S.A.   23

First edition, October 2016
Book design by Abby Dening

For Mom & Dad

CONTENTS

Chapter One

In Which We Learn That Dinosaurs Are Not Extinct

IT'S EARLY SATURDAY evening when I step inside the Good Eats 24/7 Donut Shop. The owner, Mr. Kruller, sits alone at the empty counter. He's a tall, gray-haired man who says that donuts have always been his destiny. Because Kruller.

Right now, Mr. K.'s got a white paper hat balanced on his head and a pine-green apron wrapped around his waist. He's staring at a fat paperback propped open with a half-full glass of water. "Leo Henderson," Mr. Kruller says to me without looking up from his book. "I hope you want a jelly donut."

"I—"

"Because that's all I've got. If you're looking for something different, I can't help you."

As a matter of fact, I am looking for something different. "I want—"

I'm interrupted by a familiar voice that comes from a high-backed booth in the corner. "I recommend the jelly-filleds, Leo. They're the best thing on the menu."

I peek over the top of the booth. It's my grandmother.

"They're also the only thing on the menu," she adds.

"I've heard."

Gram grins and shrugs.

I turn to Mr. Kruller. "I found what I was looking for."

He lifts the water glass, his book snaps shut, and he heads to a rack behind the counter. "I'll send your donuts over."

I move to the corner booth and slide into the seat across from Gram. She's got an old notebook, a couple *National Geographic* magazines, plus a big, unfolded road map spread in front of her. She pulls a pair of black-rimmed reading glasses off her nose and lets them dangle from a silver chain. "It took you long enough to find me."

"I wasn't looking that hard."

Gram raises an eyebrow.

"Because I knew you were here."

"What if I wasn't?" she asks.

"Then I would have looked harder."

Gram likes to wander. Finding her—at least according to my mother—is my number one chore. Generally, it's not that hard a task. My grandmother is usually walking at the park or by the river. Sometimes I find her tasting free samples at the grocery store or browsing around the Allentown Public Library. Oftentimes she just hangs out in the Good Eats 24/7 Donut Shop, where she reads or jots down her thoughts.

"How long have you been here?" I ask.

Gram glances toward the front door. Nighttime in downtown Allentown is cool and quiet and dark, but the sidewalk still holds the day's late summer heat. "It was light out when I got here."

Just then, Abbey Jones appears at our table with two fat jelly donuts on a white paper plate. She's also got a cup filled with steaming black coffee. "Hi, Leo," she says.

"Hey," I say.

When people ask, I say that Abbey is my cousin, though technically that's not true. She's actually my mother's third cousin twice removed or something like that. To me, Abbey's like a cross between a big sister, an after-school tutor, an occasional houseguest, and a slightly wacky babysitter. In any case, she works part-time for Mr. Kruller. She's seventeen, which is a few years older than me, and she's got a wide, round face and dark brown eyes. She's also got a quick temper, and wild, wavy hair that's usually twisted into a thick brown braid. Abbey's parents are divorced, so she bounces back and forth between her mom and dad. Sometimes, just because she and Mom get along more like sisters than anything else, Abbey stays at our house for a few days too. Like I said, it's easier to just say she's my cousin.

Gram accepts the coffee and cradles the cup in her hands. When she leans forward to take a sip, a few wisps of gray hair fall around her face. For a moment, Gram looks like a tiny old elf warrior, which assumes that tiny elf warriors wear drawstring pants, black high-tops, and giant fabric purses big enough to hold a potbellied pig. If all those things are true—and I hope they are—then my grandmother is the spitting image.

"This is not good coffee," Gram announces.

"It can't be that bad," says Abbey. "It's about your hundredth cup."

"No wonder you don't sleep," I say.

Gram takes another sip. "It's not the coffee that keeps me up. It's the crazy people in my house."

Abbey laughs because she knows the crazy people that Gram is talking about. It's me and my mother and, as I mentioned before, sometimes Abbey. My own parents split up right after I was born. I've never even met my dad, so Mom and I have lived in my grandparents' house for my entire life. During that time, the craziest person in the house was always my grandfather. He died about a year ago. Since then, I think we're more nuts than ever.

"Are you ready to come home?" I ask my grandmother.

"Not till I get a chocolate-sprinkled," she tells me.

"You'll have to come back tomorrow!" hollers Mr. Kruller.

Gram laughs. "Be careful what you wish for, old man!"

I point at the papers spread across the table. "What's all this?"

"Your grandmother is planning a trip," says Abbey.

Gram shakes her head. "I am not planning a trip."

"Your grandmother *should* be planning a trip," says Abbey, who turns and heads back to the kitchen.

My grandparents used to travel a lot. Mostly they took long drives to places around the U.S.A., but there haven't been any trips lately. Since Pop died, Gram hasn't gone anywhere beyond her around-town walk-abouts and wanderings. "You haven't traveled in a while," I say now.

"I've been busy," says Gram.

"Doing what?"

"Missing your grandfather. Being depressed. It takes a lot of time if you want to do it right."

My grandfather was a retired high school chemistry teacher, a crossword-puzzle master, an amazing gardener, and the ultimate math and science geek. Really, there wasn't much he didn't study or fix or figure out. Pop was constantly tinkering with everything from toaster ovens and washing machines to electrical outlets and old cars. He showed me how to build model volcanoes that actually erupt (use hydrogen peroxide, dish soap, and potassium iodide). He taught me to pick out planets from the stars (stars twinkle while planets give off a steady glow). He shared his secret for helping hot peppers grow hotter (bury a pack of matches below the seedlings, then fertilize monthly with Epsom salt), and he made me memorize multiplication tables past thirty. (There's no trick. You just have to practice.)

"I miss him too," I tell my grandmother.

Gram pushes a worn *National Geographic* my way. The magazine's cover features a small, swift-looking dinosaur racing away from an open-jawed T. rex that's just burst out of the woods. "He and I were going to drive to Utah this summer."

"What's in Utah?"

"Dinosaurs," Gram says, as if this is obvious.

"I thought they were extinct."

Gram ignores my joke. "Your grandfather wanted to visit the Cleveland-Lloyd Dinosaur Quarry. It's near a town called Price. They've found over fifteen thousand bones there, and over half of them come from allosaurs. Do you know what the word *allosaur* means, Leo?"

I shake my head.

"It means 'different lizard.' It was your grandfather's favorite dinosaur. He loved to be different."

Just then, Abbey returns with the coffeepot. "Abbey," I ask, "do you know what *allosaur* means?"

"It means 'different lizard.' It was your grandfather's favorite dinosaur." Abbey turns to Gram, then points at my grandmother's maps and magazines. "You really should go, Francine."

Abbey and Gram have been on a first-name basis since forever.

"I don't know," says Gram.

"I know," says Abbey.

"To Utah?" I say.

Abbey rolls her eyes. "That's where the allosaurs are, Leo."

"There are plenty of dinosaurs closer than that."

"But wouldn't it be awesome to see an allosaur on its home turf?" my cousin asks.

I shake my head. "You can't really see a dinosaur. They're extinct."

Abbey gives a little laugh. "Dinosaurs are all around us, Leo. Now we call them birds."

"That's just a theory."

"Gravity's just a theory, but I don't see you floating off into space." Abbey lifts the pot toward Gram. "More coffee?"

Gram puts a hand over her cup. "I think I've had enough."

"We should go home," I say.

"We should go to Utah," says Abbey.

"Home," I say again.

"Utah," Abbey repeats.

Gram holds up a hand. She looks at Abbey for a moment, turns to me, and then points at the jelly donuts on the plate between us. The glow from a green and red neon sign in the shop window makes them look like fat Christmas ornaments. "Are you going to eat those?"

I shake my head and slide the plate toward my grandmother. She devours them both. When she's done, there's a dab of white on the end of her nose. "Leo," Gram says to me, "this might be the powdered sugar talking, but I think I'd like to go to Utah."

"Seriously?" says Abbey.

"No way," I say.

"I'm in," says my cousin.

"You're not going to Utah," I tell my grandmother.

"Why not?" she asks.

"Because Mom is waiting for us at home. Because Utah is really far away. Because how would you get there anyway?"

Gram picks a set of keys off the table and dangles them in front of my face. "I have a 1973 Buick Electra parked right outside."

The old Buick is one of the projects Pop and I worked on together. That car is in better shape now than when it was new.

"You're not driving to Utah," I say a little louder than I mean to. "We have to go home."

"Leo," Gram says sweetly, "you are not the boss of me."

"She's right about that," says Abbey.

"Nobody asked you," I tell my cousin.

Gram puts a finger on the road atlas that's spread out between us. She points at a long, thin highway that's highlighted in yellow marker. "Look," she says. "Your grandfather already marked the route. From Allentown we'd head to Chicago and then cross Iowa, Nebraska, Colorado, the Rocky Mountains . . ." She looks up from her map. "We'd follow almost the exact same route as the first transcontinental railroad. Of course, they weren't concerned about dinosaurs."

I turn back and forth between my cousin and my grandmother. "This is all very interesting," I say, "but we're going home."

"I'm going to Utah," says Abbey. "Look out, allosaurs, here we come!"

Gram reaches across the table and covers my hand with her own. "Leo," she says, "you should come too."

"I can't. Neither can you. Mom would lose her mind."

Gram sighs. "Your mother enjoys losing her mind. No matter what we do or say, she is not going to let anybody take that pleasure away from her."

Gram is right about that. My mother is a preschool

teacher in Allentown's Tiny Tots Downtown Preschool. In her free time, she worries about all the ways her students are turning their brains to mush by eating glue, skipping naps, and playing video games.

"What about school?" I ask.

"School is two weeks away," says Abbey. "We're still on summer vacation. Speaking of which, have you done anything besides mope around this summer, Leo?"

"I haven't moped around."

"Have you spent any time with your friends? Have you worked on any of the projects that Pop left behind? Have you read a single book? I bet you've done nothing but hang around inside the house and miss your grandfather all summer."

"Sounds like moping to me," says Gram, "and I know moping."

"I've been doing stuff!" I protest.

"What stuff?" Abbey asks.

"I don't know. Stuff."

"I bet there's stuff in Utah," she tells me. "And it will be Utah stuff, which is much better than Pennsylvania stuff."

"I like Pennsylvania stuff." I turn to my grandmother. "You can't just hop in a car and drive to dinosaur land."

Gram stands. "I'm old, I'm able, and I've got an extremely high credit limit. Dinosaur land is definitely within my reach." She gathers up her books and magazines and maps, she slides out of the booth, and then she heads for the door.

"No," I say. "No. No. No." I sound like that annoying goldfish in *The Cat in the Hat*, but I really don't care.

"It will be an adventure!" Abbey tells me.

I ignore my cousin and follow Gram outside, where she stomps toward the big yellow Buick at the curb. Fumbling for the car keys, she drops her maps and papers. I gather everything off the ground, then jog around to the passenger side. When I get there, Gram power-locks the doors, starts the engine, and lowers the electric window a crack. "Are you coming with me?" she asks.

"I don't want an adventure," I say.

"The best adventures are always the ones you don't want."

"I want to go home."

"Say you'll come with me."

"Home, yes. Dinosaurs, no."

Gram grabs the big shift lever below the steering wheel and puts the car into gear.

"You are not leaving me here!" I try the door again. It's still locked.

"I hope not!" With that, Gram stomps on the gas. The engine roars, her tires scream, I release the door handle, and Gram tears away. I am left alone on the curb with nothing but a cloud of dust, an armful of papers, and the red-and-green glow of a blinking neon donut sign.

Chapter Two

Came We Then to the Bounds
of Deepest Water

MOM IS WAITING for me in the kitchen when I get out of bed the next morning. "Leo," she says, "tell me you know where your grandmother is." She's got her arms folded, and she's looking at me as if I'm a pre-school student with poop in his pants.

"In her room?" I suggest.

"Her car is gone." Mom pushes an envelope across the table, then runs a hand through her hair until it looks like she's got a huge tangle of blond string piled on her head. "And there's this."

I glance at the envelope. It's got my name printed

clearly across the front. It's already been ripped open. "That's supposed to be for me."

"Just read it."

After Pop died, Mom anointed herself official head of household as well as President, Principal, Queen, and Savior. Since then, I've learned that living with queens and saviors is not as much fun as you'd think. Also, presidents and principals don't believe in anybody's privacy but their own.

I lift the envelope flap and remove a small slip of paper.

"Out loud," Mom adds.

Outside, a blue morning sky promises a perfect summer day. Inside, it feels like a storm's about to break. "'Dear Leo,'" I read, "'Chocolate-sprinkles and then dinosaurs. Catch me if you can. Love, Gram.'"

"What's that supposed to mean?" asks Mom.

"I don't know."

Honestly, I'm still mad about having to walk five blocks home alone in the dark last night. I'm also a little sick of serving as a search and rescue dog, not to mention referee and translator between my mother and grandmother for the last year.

Mom sighs, but it sounds more like a growl. "She really is crazy."

"She's not crazy," I say.

"She should be in a home."

"This is a home." I point at the old appliances and the white kitchen cabinets and the Formica-topped table. "It's her home."

"This is not the kind of home I'm talking about."

I know what kind of home Mom is talking about because she collects pamphlets from nursing facilities and retirement communities, then leaves them around the house for my grandmother to see. It's a wonder that Gram hasn't hit the road sooner.

"Go get her," Mom says.

"I don't think—"

"Now."

I try to explain. "She—"

"Leo," says Mom. "Please go down to the all-night donut shop or the magic tree house or whatever secret hideout the two of you have cooked up, and bring her back. And when she gets home, I'm taking her car keys, her driver's license, and her credit card. After that, I'm either sending her to an old folks' home or locking her in the basement."

"You can't do that."

Mom shoots me a look.

"I don't think I can catch her," I say.

Mom put her hands on her hips. "Not if you're standing here, you can't."

"But—"

"Go," Mom orders. "Now. And don't come back without her."

Right then, it occurs to me that my grandmother is right. She definitely lives with crazy people. My mom is nuts for asking me to do something impossible. I'm Looney Tunes for thinking I might be able to say no. "Okay," I say to my mother. "You asked for it."

"Leo," Mom says, "I'm not asking."

"Fine." I sprint to my room, find a backpack, and stuff it with clean underwear, T-shirts, shorts, and socks. On the way back downstairs, I stop at my grandmother's room and peek inside. Her bed is made. The shades are up. Her bedside table, which usually holds a notebook, a novel or two, and a framed photo of our family, now holds nothing except Gram's cell phone, which she hates.

I step into the room, unplug the cell, and shove it into my backpack. Before I leave, I notice Pop's old binoculars on the table at his side of the bed, which makes me wonder if it's still his side of the bed now that he's dead. Either way, I take the binoculars too. When I turn back to the door, I find a Backyard Birds calendar tacked on the wall. A photo of an angry-looking goldfinch stares at me above the page for August, which is empty except for a note in Gram's tiny, neat handwriting that fills the box for August 29.

Thus with stretched sail, we went over
sea till day's end.
Sun to his slumber, shadows o'er all
the ocean,
Came we then to the bounds of deep-
est water—

The sentences are from the *Odyssey*, an old Greek poem about adventures and heroes and battles and journeys. Pop used to read sections of it out loud during the evenings. Gram's written the lines on August 29 because that's the date my grandfather died. It was a terrible day, and now the one-year anniversary is just a few days away. I didn't even realize it.

"'Came we then to the bounds of deepest water,'" I say to the stern-faced goldfinch.

The bird does not change its expression.

"Maybe you really are a dinosaur."

Still no response, so I head back downstairs. I stop in the kitchen doorway. "This might take a while," I warn my mother.

Mom crosses her arms. "Then you better get started."

I storm out of the house and start walking. I think back to a year ago and the day my grandfather died. I'd been at the park where I'd been hanging out with friends. I was drenched because we'd been playing with an old water rocket launcher that I'd built with Pop. The launcher was just plastic pipe, a bicycle pump, and some spare parts, but it could shoot a soda bottle five hundred feet high. It also got us all soaked in the process. When I got home, I was dripping wet, so I sort of expected a dirty look from Mom. I got all that and more.

"Your grandfather is dead," Mom said when I stepped through the door.

"What?"

"He had a heart attack. Your grandmother is with him at the hospital. But he's dead."

I know she was upset. Still, I wish she could have delivered the news a little more gently. But that's never been one of my mother's skills. And it's not like she's gained new abilities in the preschool classroom. If anything, she's got less patience now than ever.

Back at the Good Eats 24/7 Donut Shop, a line of Sunday morning customers snakes out the door and onto the sidewalk. I swing my pack over one shoulder and head for the entrance. "Hey, kid," somebody calls to me. "Get in line."

"I need to get my grandmother," I explain.

"I'd sell my grandmother for a cup of coffee," says the stranger.

"I'll see if that's possible." I slip inside the shop and work my way around the crowd until I'm standing at the counter.

"You're back?" Mr. Kruller asks without looking my way.

"I'm back for Gram. Is she here?"

"Does it look like she's here?" He shoves a box toward an impatient customer.

"I think she's with Abbey," I explain.

"Abbey's supposed to be at work this morning, but she's not here either." Mr. Kruller gestures at the crowd around us. "That's why this place is a madhouse."

I probably should offer to lend Mr. Kruller a hand, but I don't have time. "I want—"

Mr. K. sighs. "I know what you want, Leo." He grabs a white paper bag and fills it with a half-dozen chocolate-sprinkled donuts. "Francine was here a minute ago. She and Abbey took that giant Buick to the gas station. After they fill it up, they're coming back to wait behind the building for a little while. They're really hoping you arrive before they leave."

"I'm here!" I say.

Mr. Kruller puts the donut bag into my hand. "Then you better get going."

"Excuse me," a customer calls. "Are there any chocolate-sprinkled left?"

Mr. Kruller nods at me. "This kid just took the last one."

"Awwwww!" moans the crowd.

"Better use the back door," Mr. Kruller tells me.

I hold up the donuts. "Thank you!"

I make my way around the counter, then cut through the donut kitchen until I spot a big green door beneath a bright red EXIT sign. I shove the door open and step into a hot, narrow alley that runs between the back sides of two brick buildings. Other than some broken cardboard boxes and a couple squat garbage bins, nothing's back here. No Abbey. No Gram. No Buick.

"I'm here," I say to nobody.

Before I can decide what to do next, the deep thrum of a big-block engine growls in the distance. A moment later, just like Mr. Kruller promised, the long yellow Buick skids around the corner, then roars down the alley. The car's got fins on its tail, chrome on the hubcaps, and Gram behind the steering wheel. Abbey waves at me from the passenger seat while Gram brings the Electra to a screeching halt.

"Leo," Abbey yells through her open window, "you almost missed the boat!"

"But you didn't!" shouts Gram. "All aboard!" She opens her door, but before I can climb in, a giant golden retriever leaps out of the car and into my arms. I take a step back, trip over my own feet, and land on my rear end. I try to stand, but the dog, who is the same yellow-gold color as the Buick, starts licking my face as if I'm made out of vanilla ice cream.

"Leo," says Abbey, who has stepped out of the car, "you know Kermit. He's coming with us." Kermit the dog has been with Abbey for as long as I can remember. I didn't think about it, but of course there's no way Abbey would leave Kermit behind.

I stand, wipe golden retriever slobber off my face, then grab my backpack and the paper donut bag off the ground. I shove the donuts toward Gram. "Here," I tell her.

Gram opens the bag, pulls out a chocolate-sprinkled, and takes a big bite. "Now," she says through a mouth filled with donut, "we've got everything we need to put this show on the road."

"We're going to need more than donuts," I say.

Gram laughs. "I guess we'll see about that."

Chapter Three

In Which Dinosaurs Prove That Nothing Is Ever Dead and Gone

GRAM BRINGS US out of the alleyway and through Allentown. As she steers toward the highway, I consider my situation: I'm in my dead grandfather's car with a runaway grandma, a nutty cousin, and a lion-size golden retriever who's named after a talking frog. We're about to drive across America, and my mother expects me home for supper. I should probably call and say I'm going to be late, but I'm sure I'll never get a word in past "hello." On top of everything else, Kermit has really bad breath. He's seriously gassy too.

"What do you feed this dog?" I ask Abbey.

"Dog food," she tells me. "There's a big bag in the trunk."

"He doesn't smell like dog food."

"You don't smell so good yourself, Leo."

Kermit pants and gives me a grin. More than half of him is in my lap, which wouldn't be so bad if it wasn't his back half. "Where are we going first?" I ask.

"The Windy City," says Gram. "Chi-Town. Paris on the Prairie. The Miracle Mile." She breaks into song. *"Chicago! Chicago! That toddlin' town!"*

"And then allosaurs after that?"

Abbey turns in her seat to face me. "It's seven hundred miles from here to Chicago. It's another fifteen hundred miles to Utah. It's going to take a few days to get from here to there."

"We are setting sail on a journey of epic proportions," announces Gram. "We're like Odysseus and Jacques Cousteau, Marco Polo and Amelia Earhart, Edmund Hillary and Nellie Bly, Sally Ride and Sacagawea, Ibn Battuta and Neil Armstrong."

"Ibby what?" asks Abbey.

"Ibn," says Gram. "Rhymes with 'ribbon.' He was a

fourteenth-century Muslim traveler and writer. Ibn Battuta is known around the world as one of the greatest explorers of all time."

"I've never heard of him," I admit.

"Then your world is too small," Gram tells me. "Luckily, we're about to fix that."

I glance outside. We've passed a mishmash set of turret-topped row houses, the Allentown farmers' market, and the redbrick Church of St. Catharine of Siena. "I like my world," I say.

Gram runs a hand through her hair. "Believe it or not," she says, "the universe continues beyond the edge of Allentown."

"Excuse me," says Abbey.

"Yes?" says Gram.

Abbey points up ahead. "Red light!"

Gram stomps hard on the brakes. We jerk to a halt at an intersection that's just a block away from the highway on-ramp.

"We've got four thousand miles to go," says Abbey. "Let's not wreck the car just yet."

Gram glances in the rearview mirror and gives me a grin. "There's nothing we can't fix. Right, Leo?"

I don't know about that, but before I can say so, the signal light changes.

"Green light," says Abbey.

Gram punches the gas. The Electra leaps forward. Kermit and I are pressed into the backseat, and we blast through the intersection.

"We're off!" says Gram.

"Woof!" says Kermit.

Abbey laughs. "Look out, Utah! Here we come!"

Right now, I'll be happy if we make it out of Pennsylvania alive.

—

Somehow, between bathroom breaks, dog walks, food stops, and adrenaline, our first day on the road goes quickly. We pass the WELCOME TO OHIO sign before I know it. "You should call your mom," says Abbey as we enter the Buckeye State.

"And tell her what?" I ask.

"That you're not dead. That she shouldn't call the police. That you won't be home for supper. You know," says Abbey. "The basics."

I reach into my backpack, pull out the binoculars, then find Gram's cell, which I hand to my cousin. "You call her."

Gram's eyes narrow when she sees the phone. "I left that behind for a reason."

"It won't hurt to have it with us," I say.

Gram shakes her head. "Those things are like talking to a rock and listening to a seashell. It's half robot babysitter, half do-it-yourself lobotomy, half spy satellite, and half prescription for stupid."

"That's a lot of halves," I say.

Abbey pushes the phone back at me. "I have my own."

Gram pulls onto the shoulder of the road and brings the Buick to a stop. "I'll call her." She takes her cell, then taps at the screen like she's defusing a bomb. A moment later, she's shouting into the handset. "Jules! It's your mother! Pick up if you're there!"

"Hi, Auntie Julie!" Abbey yells at the phone.

Gram waves Abbey away. "Listen up!" she continues. "Leo is with me. He's fine. I'm fine. Everything's fine. We'll call again tomorrow. Or maybe the next day. Don't worry. I'm not kidnapping him or anything." She's about to hang up but then adds, "And Abbey too." With that, Gram ends the call.

"What kind of message is that?" I ask.

Gram hands the phone back to me. "Hopefully it's the kind that prevents your mother from having a panic attack."

I lift the binoculars to my face and stare into the dark. "Have you met my mother?"

Gram shoots me a look in the rearview mirror. "Your grandfather's field glasses!" she exclaims. "I knew I forgot something."

The binoculars, which are dented and scratched, were one of Pop's prize possessions. They're engraved U.S. NAVY BUREAU OF SHIPS 1942, which means, at least according to my grandfather, that they definitely saw some kind of battle action somewhere. Whatever they went through, they're still great binoculars.

Gram glances over her shoulder to make sure her lane is clear, then pulls back onto the highway. "Leo," she says, "put the binoculars away and close your eyes for a while."

It's dark outside, but I'm not tired. "It's barely nine o'clock."

"I've got a couple more hours of driving in me," Gram says. "Then it's Abbey's turn behind the wheel. I want you to stay awake and keep her company. You don't have to sleep. Just get some rest."

I can't believe I fall for the old you-don't-have-to-go-to-sleep-just-close-your-eyes-and-get-some-rest trick. I return the binoculars to my backpack, lean back in the seat, and then pass out in no time. When I wake up, Kermit is on his back with all four paws in the air. Abbey is snoring up front. Gram's got the radio turned low, and she's singing along with some old dead rock-and-roll hero. "Where are we?" I ask.

"Maybe Cleveland?" Gram says.

Outside, it's pitch-black. "I thought there'd be more to Cleveland than this."

Abbey sits up and wipes an arm across her face. "What?" she says groggily.

"Welcome to Cleveland," I tell her.

"I think we're actually closer to Toledo." Gram stretches one arm and rubs her eyes. "I also think I'm getting tired."

"Pull over at the next rest stop," Abbey tells her. "We'll let Kermit pee, and then I'll drive."

As it works out, the golden retriever isn't the only animal in this car who has to pee. Once we pile back into the Buick, Gram takes the backseat with Kermit, and I sit up front with Abbey. We're barely on the road again before Gram and the dog are both snoring loudly.

"If you want your driver to stay awake, you better make some conversation," Abbey instructs me.

I turn and look out the window. "Ohio sure is dark."

"That's scintillating," says Abbey.

"And flat," I add.

Abbey peers over the steering wheel into the dark. "How can you tell?"

I point out the front window. "The stars reach all the way to the horizon." Except for an occasional tree, the starry sky drapes down around us like it's painted inside an upside-down cereal bowl that's been placed on top of the world.

Abbey rests her chin on the steering wheel and peers up through the windshield. "You're right. I hadn't noticed that."

I lean forward and stare outside too. "I've never been this far from home."

"Do you feel any different?" Abbey asks.

I think about the question. "I miss my grandfather."

"Don't you miss him when you're at home too?"

"Yeah."

"So what's the difference?"

I shrug. "At home it always feels like maybe he's just in the other room."

"But you know he's not."

"Sometimes I forget."

"By accident or on purpose?"

"What do you mean?"

Abbey waits to respond until a couple long trucks pass us on the left. They make the Buick shudder as they roar by. "He's hardly been gone a year, Leo."

"So?"

"So it doesn't seem like something you'd forget."

I turn my face away and stare into the darkness. "I don't really forget."

Abbey sighs. "Me neither."

"Can we change the subject?" I ask.

Abbey leans away from the steering wheel. "Go for it."

"Why are you here?"

The light from the dashboard illuminates Abbey's face in a soft, pretty glow. "That's a big question, Leo."

"I mean, why are you in this car? Why are you on this trip? Why did you want to take a ride to Utah?"

"Oh," says Abbey. "That's easy." She turns to face me. "Littlefoot."

"Excuse me?"

"Littlefoot was the baby long-neck dinosaur in *The Land Before Time* cartoon," she explains. "He was my favorite character, and then one day your grandfather told me that dinosaurs are real. Actually real! From there, the rest is history. Or maybe it's prehistory. In any case, I want to be a paleontologist."

"Seriously?"

"Dinosaurs are awesome, Leo. They're bigger than life, but they actually existed. They dominated the world, and we hardly know anything about them. They were everywhere, and now they're almost invisible."

"That's because they're dead and gone."

Abbey shakes her head. "Dinosaurs prove that nothing is ever really dead and gone."

I stare out the window and watch the occasional silhouettes of trees and barns drift by. I wonder if one day my cousin will discover great secrets about our planet's ancient past because once upon a time she fell in love with a cartoon dinosaur. "Did you tell your parents you were going to Utah?"

"I told them that I'd be watching you for a few days."

"I'm too old to need a babysitter," I say.

"I know," says Abbey, "but I'm not too old to need an alibi."

I glance in the backseat at my sleeping grandmother. "Are we really doing this just to see some dinosaurs?"

Abbey laughs. "Leo, I'm pretty sure that I'm the only one in this car who really cares about dinosaurs."

Chapter Four

Enormous, Colossal, Astonishing, Dumbfounding, Terrifying, Extraordinary, Incredible

I WAKE UP with the sun blasting inside the car and Gram banging on the Buick's passenger-side door. Since she is outside, I deduce that we are no longer moving down the highway. "Leo!" Gram calls. "Breakfast!"

I sit up. "Where are we?"

Gram lifts a white cardboard donut box in one hand and a paper coffee cup in the other. She starts singing and doing a little dance in her high-tops. *"Sweet home, Chicago!"*

I open the car door, put my feet onto a warm sidewalk, and look around from the front seat. Gram shoves the donuts in my face, so I take a chocolate-sprinkled.

It's good but not as good as the ones at home. "Where did these come from?"

"We went through a drive-thru," Gram tells me. "You were fast asleep. Did you know you look like your father when you're asleep?"

Abbey's walking Kermit on a patch of grass a couple yards away. That doesn't stop her head from swiveling around like she's been hit by a brick. Neither she nor I have ever heard Gram talk about my father.

"What do you know about your father?" Gram asks me now.

Even if I was wide awake and my mouth wasn't filled with donut, it would be hard to speak. My father is just not a thing that's talked about. "I know he left right after I was born."

"Anything else?"

I swallow the big wad of donut that's caught in my throat. "He and Mom met in college. Mom left school to have me. I think my father played basketball. Or maybe volleyball. Something with a ball."

Gram nods. "His dream was to play volleyball in Italy."

"He left us for Italian volleyball?"

Gram shakes her head. "He left because he was just a kid. He was no more ready to be a father and husband than you are right now."

I wipe donut crumbs off my face. "Why are you telling me this?"

"I've been worried that nobody else is going to do it. That would leave a pretty big hole for you to fill." Gram takes a sip from her coffee. "I'll tell you more if you want."

I glance toward Abbey. She gives me a shrug.

"I'll let you know," I tell Gram.

"Sounds good." She waves an arm in the direction of the sun. "Did you see Lake Michigan? I can't believe they call that thing a lake."

"What else would they call it?" asks Abbey.

"An inland sea," says Gram.

I stand so I can check things out for myself. A few hundred yards away, a huge body of water stretches in front of us. In the distance, a few ships—a couple fat oil tankers, a three-masted sailing ship, and a couple long, flat-topped barges—seem to be making their way across the horizon. Gram is right. This is no ordinary lake. Lakes are where Pop took me fishing for bluegills and bass that fit in a frying pan. This is where you'd go to harpoon whales and dragons and sea monsters.

"Ready to see some dinosaurs?" Gram asks.

"Here?" I ask.

She points across the street. "There."

Together we head toward a building that looks like it belongs on the back of a million-dollar bill. It's as if some ancient Roman or Greek temple got dropped into the middle of America when nobody was looking. There's even a set of stone goddesses on either side of the white columns that surround the building's entryway.

"Welcome to the world-famous Field Museum," Gram tells me.

I point at the statues. "Are those guards?"

"Those are *caryatids*," Gram explains.

"They don't look like bugs to me."

"Not katydids," Gram says. "Caryatids. Katydids are related to crickets. Caryatids are ancient Spartan women carved out of stone. You don't want to mess around with Spartan women, Leo."

I recall the Greek myths that Pop used to share. When a Spartan man went to war, his mother would hand him his shield and say, "With it or on it." In other words, come back a winner or come back dead. "I bet Spartan women would not make good dog sitters," I say.

"I think not," says Gram.

"That's too bad because I bet they're not going to let us bring a golden retriever into a museum filled with gigantic bones."

Gram turns toward Kermit. "I hadn't thought of that," she admits.

"Woof!" says Kermit as if he understands.

"How about this?" Abbey suggests. "You two go in and visit the dinosaurs. I'll stay outside with Kermit for now. Then one of you can come out and switch places with me in about an hour. We'll take turns."

Gram nods. "That works for me."

"Me too," I say.

"Woof!" Kermit says again.

"Perfect," says Abbey. "I'll see one of you in an hour." She leads Kermit away on his leash, and Gram and I head toward the Field Museum.

"Thanks for telling me something about my dad,"

I say to Gram as we climb the long stairs leading to the museum. "Are there any other family secrets I should know about?" I ask only half joking.

"Well," says Gram, "there's Peter."

"Who's Peter?"

"He would be your uncle, though it's hard to think of him as anybody's uncle. He died when he was very young." Gram hesitates, then gives me a forced-looking smile. "He's still a little boy to me."

I stop at the top step. "Wait a minute. I have an uncle? Mom had a brother?"

Gram nods while she pauses to catch her breath.

"First you tell me my dad is an Italian volleyballer, and now I've got a secret uncle?"

Gram shrugs. "You asked."

"How come I've never heard about Peter before?"

"Your mother and your grandfather could never talk about it. And then it became a sort of rule in the house. Nobody was allowed to talk about Peter."

"Ever?"

"Never."

"Was it the same rule for my father?"

Gram shakes her head. "We hardly even knew your father. There's not much to talk about."

I don't know if that should make me feel better or worse.

Gram joins me on the top step, then points at a caryatid. "Did you know that the Spartans only ever put your name on a gravestone if you died in battle or if you died in childbirth?"

I don't say anything.

"I never thought that was right," Gram continues. "Just being alive—even if you're only on the planet for a few years—is struggle enough. You've earned the right to be remembered."

"What happened to Mom's brother?" I ask.

A surprisingly strong breeze blows off the lake and pushes Gram back a step. I offer her my arm, but she leans against a nearby railing to steady herself. "Everybody called him Peter the Great. He and Julie were playing catch. Peter was the younger of the two. He chased the ball into the street."

"Oh."

"It was an accident."

I don't really know what to say. I feel terrible for my mom and my grandparents, but I've got some questions. And I think I deserve some answers. "Is that why Mom is so—"

"Leo," Gram says, "not many people get over something like that."

I study my grandmother for a moment. "Ever?"

She shakes her head. "It just becomes a part of who you are."

The two of us stand quietly and study the big lake and the Chicago skyline for a little while. As quickly as it blew in, the wind has died down now. "Listen," Gram says matter-of-factly, "it was a terrible time. It was the end of the world, but guess what? The world didn't end. The world keeps going. For a while, I was very angry about that."

"That the world didn't end?"

Gram nods. "I feel differently about it now. We were lucky to have Peter for as long as we did. That's how I feel today, and I will tell you more stories about Peter if you'd like."

"And my father?"

"And your father, but first"—she points at the Field Museum—"how about we check out some dinosaurs?"

Gram doesn't seem distraught or anything. I guess it's because she's already been living with this for years and years. Still, it's clear that she'd like our conversation about the past to end. At least for now. And even though I'd like to hear more about this uncle I've never heard of and this father we never talk about, I nod. "Okay."

Together, Gram and I head through the museum doors. Inside, a pretty girl greets us from behind the ticket counter. "Welcome to the Field Museum!" She says it as if we've just won the lottery. Behind her, a massive T. rex skeleton looms over an open space that's as long as a football field and as high as a cathedral.

"Wow!" I say.

The girl glances back over her shoulder, then turns back to give me a big grin. "I know!" She's got long dark hair, and she's wearing a museum staff shirt that reveals intricate, flowing Filipino tattoos that start somewhere above her short sleeves and reach almost to her wrists. I know the tattoos are Filipino because a neat, hand-printed notecard on the counter says:

*Hi! The tattoos, which cover my entire back,
shoulders, and upper arms, are traditional
Filipino tribal designs. It did hurt. My
parents don't mind. I am proudly Filipina
and American. I was born in Nebraska.
I study paleontology at the University of
Nebraska. Thank you for asking.*

IN NATURE THERE'S NO BLEMISH BUT THE MIND;
NONE CAN BE CALLED DEFORMED BUT THE UNKIND.
            —William Shakespeare

Gram points at the card, then addresses the girl, whose name tag identifies her as Honey Buenafe. "Honey," says Gram, "what's that about?"

"The quote?" the girl asks.

"The whole thing," says Gram.

Honey Buenafe shrugs, then smiles. "I love Shakespeare, and I get tired of answering the same questions every day. I guess I'm killing two birds with one stone."

"Like Hamlet says," Gram tells her, "'Oh, 'tis most sweet when in one line two crafts directly meet.'"

"Exactly!" Honey hands us our entrance tickets, and we see another tattoo. This one is on the inside of her wrist. It's a tiny, remarkably detailed image of a dinosaur fossil.

"Wow!" says Gram. *Wow* seems to be an important word at the Field Museum, and we're barely inside the door. Gram points at the tattoo. "Where do you get one of those?"

"You are not getting a tattoo," I tell my grandmother.

"I'm studying to be a paleontologist," says Honey.

Gram points at the card. "I know."

Honey grins. "Right. I worked on a dig last summer, and on the way home, I found a tattoo artist in Denver who did this for me."

Gram studies the tattoo. "We could stop in Denver," she suggests to me.

"We're not stopping in Denver," I warn my grandmother. I turn to Honey. "We're going to Utah. We're going to see allosaurs."

Honey's eyes light up. "The Different Lizard. They're my favorite!" She holds out her wrist so that Gram and I can examine her dinosaur tattoo more closely. "This is an allosaur."

"It is?" I lean forward to examine the little fossil design, which doesn't look anything like the intricate tribal decorations visible on the rest of Honey's skin. "What's it doing?"

"It's not doing anything," Honey says. "It's dead. This is a death pose. It's how a real allosaur fossil might look if you found a whole one in stone."

"Death pose?" says Gram.

Honey nods. "Birds and dinosaur fossils are often found this way with their head thrown back, the spine arched, the tail extended, and the mouth wide open. Nobody really knows why."

I examine Honey's dinosaur tattoo. "It kind of looks alive."

She nods. "I think it looks like it's dancing."

"People say a lot of stuff about the afterlife," says Gram. "I definitely hope there's dancing."

"But first you should check out the museum," Honey suggests.

Gram waves our admission tickets in the air. "I like the way you think, Honey Buenafe."

Honey gives us a grin. "Have fun!"

Gram takes my hand like I'm four years old and

drags me into the building. We head straight toward the Tyrannosaurus rex, which, according to several large banners, is named Sue.

"Wow," Gram says again.

"We have to come up with a new word," I tell her.

But really, words are too small for the thing that is in front of us. It's enormous, colossal, astonishing, dumbfounding, terrifying, extraordinary, incredible. . . . Tyrannosaurus Sue is over forty feet long with jaws that hover a dozen feet over my head. Imagining what this creature must have been like in real life makes me dizzy. How is it even possible that I am alive on the same planet that was once home to this creature?

"Come on," Gram says to me.

"Huh?"

She shakes an open museum map at me. "There's more! And we want to let Abbey have a turn."

Before I can speak, we're heading down one set of stairs, then up another. We go past stuffed gorillas and two stuffed lions called the Tsavo Man-Eaters. "Are they real?" I ask, but Gram keeps pulling me along. We squeeze through a damp tomb filled with stone caskets and Egyptian mummies. We pass display cases stuffed with medieval weapons and strange shoes and Native American headdresses. I am now totally dazed and disoriented.

Gram points to a marble staircase. "That way." We climb the steps and come out in the grand hallway where we began. Gram points at two life-size elephants mounted a few feet away from Tyrannosaurus Sue. "Were those elephants there when we started?"

I nod.

Gram rubs her forehead. "This place is sort of overwhelming."

She sounds out of breath and a little confused. Between chasing after Gram, running away from home, driving all night, not to mention learning about a secret, dead uncle, I'm a little confused too. "Do you want to sit down for a minute?"

Gram shakes her head. "Your grandfather is waiting for us outside."

"You mean Abbey and Kermit."

She rolls her eyes. "What am I talking about? Your grandfather is dead. Sometimes I forget he's gone."

"You do?"

"Don't you?" Gram asks.

"All the time," I admit.

"It stinks, doesn't it? When you remember, it's like losing him all over again." Before I can reply, Gram points at a water fountain. "That's what I really need. Dehydration is not good for an old lady, Leo." After a long drink, she glances up at the elephants. "I wonder if it's true that elephants never forget."

"That's something Pop would know."

"And he probably told me." Gram begins to laugh. "But I forget. Now how about we head for the dinosaurs?"

"I'm going to ask for directions," I tell my grandmother.

She grins. "Or you could just look behind you."

I turn and find a sign with an arrow pointing at a nearby stairwell. I read it out loud. "'Dinosaurs This Way.'"

There's a crowd on the stairs, which is a good thing because it forces Gram and me to move slowly and catch our breath. By the time we reach the second floor, we've been pushed apart, which is not a big deal because we can still see each other. Also, it's clear that we're all heading to the same place. The small mob rolls toward a doorway that's as wide as the opening to a stone-arched train tunnel. Above the entrance, it says HALL OF DINOSAURS.

Somehow I've been jammed by the crowd into a big family with small children. One of the kids, a little girl who looks like she's no more than five or six years old, is smiling like she's about to burst. "This is going to be so great," she is saying to nobody in particular. "This is going to be so great!" Without thinking, she grabs my hand and shouts. "THIS IS GOING TO BE SO GREAT!"

We reach the door that leads into the hall of dinosaurs. We step inside, and the little girl stops as if she's just stuck her feet into quicksand. We are surrounded by dozens and dozens of mounted fossils. Several carnivores lean toward us. A long-necked sauropod reaches toward a far wall, and a couple pterodactyls hang from the ceiling. The girl cups both her hands into a megaphone around her mouth. She takes a big breath and hollers at the top of her lungs.

"THIS. IS. AWESOME!!!!!"

She is absolutely right. And not just because of the giant monster skeletons assembled all around us. In this room, these long-dead creatures—triceratopses, stegosaurs, brontosauruses, deinonychuses, archaeopteryxes, compsognathuses, hadrosaurs, pteranodons, and more—are alive and well. In here, they still roam and roar and rule the earth.

Of course, none of this has been true for millions and millions of years, but in here, the past is real. And somehow that makes yesterday—a time when my grandfather was still with us, a time when Mom played ball, a time when there was a boy named Peter—seem not so far away.

Chapter Five

What to Do When Your Grandmother's About to Turn into a Man-Eating Lion

TRYING TO SPEND an hour inside the Hall of Dinosaurs is like trying to eat a glacier with a teaspoon. There's just too much. I turn to Gram, who's marveling at a gigantic sea monster that's mounted on the wall above us. "I'm going to trade places with Abbey."

"Already?" Gram asks.

"It's been over an hour."

Gram raises an eyebrow. "In that case, you better go." She knows that dinosaurs are more Abbey's thing than mine, which means that my cousin is probably about to explode.

I head back the way we came. I pass the Tsavo

Man-Eaters and the elephants and Tyrannosaurus Sue. Finally, I find the entrance we used earlier. Right outside, Abbey and Kermit are sitting midway up the long white staircase that leads to the museum. Abbey's got her phone in her hand, but I'm surprised to see that she's talking with the tattooed girl from the front desk.

"Hey!" I call.

"Leo!" Abbey shoves the phone into her pocket. "Come here! I want you to meet someone!"

I jog down the steps.

"This is Honey Buenafe," Abbey says. "She's going to be a paleontologist."

Honey smiles. "So are you," she tells my cousin.

"We already met," I say.

Honey nods. "At the ticket counter."

But Honey is no longer wearing her Field Museum uniform. Now she's in a pair of loose cotton pants plus an oversize T-shirt that shows a blue-haired cartoon boy on the front and the words HOPIA MANI POPCORN across the back.

"Are you on a break?" I ask.

Honey shakes her head. "I only work at the Field Museum during the summer. My last day was actually yesterday. I just came in this morning to help out for a couple hours, but now I'm officially unemployed. I have to be back in class next week."

"At the University of Nebraska," says Abbey.

"I know." I point at the HOPIA MANI POPCORN slogan on Honey's shirt. "Is that a Filipino snack food?"

"Good guess," Honey tells me. "But it's Filipino rock and roll."

"Leo's more interested in snack foods," says Abbey.

"That's true," I admit.

"We're going to give Honey a ride home," Abbey informs me.

"Oh?"

"She was going to take a bus, but Nebraska's on our way."

"As long as you don't mind," says Honey.

I shrug. It's better than stopping in Denver for tattoos. "It's okay with me."

I'm about to suggest that Abbey head inside to join Gram in the Hall of Dinosaurs when I notice some commotion across the street. A gigantic purple tow truck just stopped alongside our Buick. The truck driver hops out of his cab, which forces traffic to go around him. Meanwhile, a burly police officer who looks like a square blue LEGO block with a head stands with one foot on the Electra's back bumper.

"Uh-oh," I say.

"What?" asks Abbey.

"Go get Gram."

Abbey turns and follows my gaze toward the street.

"Isn't that your car?" Honey asks.

I take Kermit's leash. "Gram's in the Hall of Dinosaurs," I tell my cousin. "Run!"

Honey takes Abbey's arm. "I know a shortcut."

The two girls sprint into the museum, leaving me and Kermit to deal with the LEGO cop and the purple tow truck. With Kermit at my side, I head to the curb. A line of traffic prevents us from crossing the street. "Excuse me!" I shout across the road at the police officer.

The policeman can't hear or else he's just ignoring me.

"Hey! Hello!"

I get no answer.

"Could you please wait a minute?" I holler.

Still no response. Meanwhile, the tow truck guy

heads to the back of his rig and begins yanking on a couple long levers. A big winch clunks and whines, then lowers a set of cables to attach to our car.

"Oh no you don't," I mutter. Quickly, I pull on Kermit's leash, and we both step into traffic.

The sudden sound of tires screeching and horns blasting gets the cop's attention. It's his turn to yell. "What do you think you're doing?!"

I ignore the police officer and head straight for the tow truck operator. "Don't," I tell him.

"Woof!" says Kermit.

The man stops the winch and steps back. He holds his hands up like this is a stickup.

"You can't tow this car," I tell him.

"Hey, kid," LEGO cop calls to me.

I turn to the officer. "That's my grandmother's car."

The policeman points at a red-and-white sign mounted on a shiny metal pole just a few feet away from the Buick. "This is a no-parking zone."

I look up at the sign. It's got a little picture of a car getting pulled away by a tow truck. I guess we should have noticed that. The officer even reads the sign out loud for me. "'No parking any time.'"

I can't argue, so I decide to go for sympathy. "My grandfather died a year ago. The Field Museum was his favorite place in the world. We drove my grandmother here all the way from Allentown, Pennsylvania, so she could see it one last time."

The policeman shakes his head.

"She's partially blind," I throw in. "And she's sick." I know I shouldn't lie, but I'm desperate. "Plus, she's a little demented."

"She has dementia?" says the officer.

I try to look and sound as pitiful as possible. "Please don't leave us here without a car."

The tow guy drops to one knee, then reaches out toward Kermit, who ambles over for a scratch behind his ears. "I got a golden retriever at home," he says in a thick Chicago accent. "D'yuh know who goldens love best?"

"Who?" I ask.

"Whoever they're looking at."

Kermit leans forward and starts to lick the driver's face. Based on his big grin—the man's, not Kermit's— this guy definitely loves dogs. "How 'bout this?" he says to the police officer. "I go and grab us some coffees. If there's a car here when I get back, then I tow it. If not, then I don't. Either way, you get a cup of coffee. What do you think?"

Officer LEGO considers the suggestion, then snaps his notebook shut. "I could use a coffee."

"Thank you," I say.

The tow operator stands and heads back to his truck, where he rewinds the winch. A moment later, he hops into his cab. "Hope I don't see you soon!" he shouts at me as he pulls away from the curb.

Meanwhile, the police officer has returned his pad to a pocket. I notice that he's got a lot of pockets. In fact, he's got a lot of everything. Besides a gold badge and a walkie-talkie clipped to his shirt, the officer's got handcuffs, a black nightstick, a bulletproof vest, a silver flashlight, and a very large holster, which contains a very large gun. Basically, he's a big blue Swiss Army Knife with firepower. I point at his gun. "Do you ever have to use that?"

"I try to avoid it."

"But sometimes?"

"My sister is a middle school teacher. She sees more blood in a week than I do in a year."

Somehow that's not reassuring.

A moment later, Gram, Abbey, and Honey Buenafe burst out of the museum. Gram's in the lead as they sprint down the stairs, dodge traffic, and join me on the sidewalk beside our car. "Are you okay?" Gram asks after she catches her breath.

The officer steps forward. "Is this your grandmother?" he asks me.

I nod.

"She moves pretty fast for somebody on her deathbed."

"She's not really dying," I say.

"Just blind?"

"More like visually impaired."

"What's he talking about?" Gram asks.

I point at the NO PARKING sign.

Gram looks up, then puts a hand to her forehead. "I can't believe I didn't see that."

I turn to the policeman. "See what I mean?"

Gram reaches into her purse and pulls out the car keys. I snatch them away and toss them to Abbey. "What'd you do that for?" Gram asks.

"She doesn't drive anymore," I assure the police officer.

Gram puts a hand on one hip. "What are you talking about?"

Abbey dangles the car keys in front of her as if she's holding a dead mouse. She nods toward the gigantic Buick. "I am not driving this battleship through the city."

"I am perfectly capable—" Gram begins.

I cut her off. "Of course you are." I shoot a look at the police officer and roll my eyes as if I think Gram's crazy. From there, I step forward and put a hand on my grandmother's arm. "Gram," I say, "it's Honey's turn to drive."

"Honey?"

"She's coming with us."

"She is?"

I glance at the police officer. "She gets confused."

Gram turns and punches me in the arm. "I am confused because this conversation is confusing."

The police officer's eyes narrow. He's quickly losing his patience. "Here's what I suggest," he says. "Somebody move this car right now."

"Honey will do it." I glance at the tattooed girl. "Okay?"

"Sure," she says.

I step toward Abbey, take the keys, and hand them to Honey.

"Thank you for visiting Chicago," the police officer tells us. "Be sure to come again . . . when I'm off duty."

"Wait a minute," says Abbey. "I hardly saw any dinosaurs."

"I'm taking the week off after Thanksgiving," says the cop. "Come back then."

I ignore him, open the car door, and help Kermit and Gram into the backseat. Abbey takes the front, and Honey gets behind the wheel.

"Somebody better tell me what's going on," Gram says in a voice that sounds like she's about to turn into one of the Tsavo man-eating lions.

"We're going to Nebraska," I tell her.

"When?" she asks.

"Do you know the way out of here?" I ask Honey.

"Sure," she tells me.

I turn to Gram. "Right now."

Chapter Six

How to Strip the Flesh Off Squirrel Nutkin

I'VE BARELY GOT the back door closed when Honey steps on the gas and the car leaps forward. "This thing's got power!" Honey says.

"Be careful!" says Gram.

"Get down!" hollers Abbey.

I duck down in the back, but then I realize Abbey isn't talking to me. She's talking to Kermit. The dog's got two paws on the front seat, and he's shoving his nose into Honey's black hair as if she's got a tennis ball hiding in there. Honey laughs. "It's okay. I like dogs."

Gram reaches forward and pulls Kermit back until he settles on the backseat. "I don't mean to be rude," she says, "but can somebody tell me why a girl we hardly know is driving us to Nebraska in our car?"

Honey bites her lip and glances at Abbey.

Abbey turns and faces the backseat. "I can explain."

"Please do," Gram says.

"Honey's from Nebraska."

Gram nods. "I know that."

"Nebraska is on the way to Utah."

"I know where Nebraska is."

"She needs a ride home, so I said we'd take her."

Gram studies Abbey for a long moment. "Okay," she finally says. "That's all fine. But why is she behind the wheel?"

"I don't really know," Abbey admits.

"I'm kind of curious about that myself," says Honey, who's steered us into a line of slow-moving traffic that's heading toward the Chicago skyline.

Gram turns to me. "Leo?"

"Our car was about to get towed," I explain.

"I could have moved it," says Gram.

I shake my head. "They were getting ready to take it before you got outside."

"I didn't see any tow truck," Gram says. "I just saw

that policeman. Did anybody else think that guy was shaped like a brick?"

"The tow truck left," I explain. "I talked them out of it."

"How did you do that?"

I glance outside. Slowly but surely, Honey is moving us across Chicago. We've passed sailboats and fountains, stadiums and skyscrapers. "I told them we'd come a long way."

"And then he just let you go?" asks Gram.

"The tow truck guy liked golden retrievers."

Abbey reaches over the backseat and rubs Kermit's head. "Of course he did."

Gram crosses her arms. "That's a pretty nice tow truck driver."

"I also told the policeman that we were making this trip for our grandmother."

Gram says nothing, so I continue.

"Who was old and sick and blind and crazy."

The car fills with a sudden, uncomfortable silence.

"I don't like that," Gram finally says. "I don't like that at all."

"But you're not any of those things," I tell her.

"Leo, I get enough of that from your mother."

"But I had to save the car."

"Next time," she says, "let them take it."

We ride without speaking for a long time. Honey brings us to an on-ramp that leads to the expressway. A few minutes later, we're leaving Chicago behind.

"So," Abbey says to Honey Buenafe, "where in Nebraska are we going?"

"Nebraska City, Nebraska," Honey tells us.

"Is that like New York City, New York?"

Honey laughs. "Not quite." She glances in the rear-view mirror at Gram and me. "Are you really going to Utah just to see some allosaurs?"

"That's why I'm going," says Abbey.

I nod at my grandmother. "I'm going because she's going."

Gram has her back to me. She's staring out the window. "I'm going because they made me." Outside, cornfields and billboards and long strings of telephone wire line the highway while white clouds the size of small planets float above us. "I wouldn't mind stopping in Denver to get one of those allosaur tattoos," she adds.

"You are not getting a tattoo." I wonder if I'm the first kid in America who's had to say that to his grandma several times in one day.

A few hours later, I sit up with a start. I remember a rest stop in the middle of Illinois, but I must have fallen asleep after that. Honey is still behind the wheel. The sun is setting, and Abbey and Gram are both snoring loudly.

I lean forward so that my head is between Honey and my sleeping cousin. I point outside at a huge body of water beneath the bridge we're crossing. "Is that another Great Lake?"

"That's the Mississippi River," Honey tells me.

"*The* Mississippi River?" I ask.

"There's only one," she says.

Around us, traffic is going back and forth without much fanfare. Drivers in nearby cars are focused on the road except for a couple people who are tapping at their phones. I point at one guy who is texting while he passes us. "That's stupid."

Honey nods toward another driver who has a newspaper propped on her steering wheel. "You don't need a cell phone in order to be dangerous and dumb."

Meanwhile, the huge river slides beneath us. "We're really crossing the Mississippi?" I ask.

Honey grins. "Pretty cool, huh?"

I rub my eyes, then study the drivers around us. "Nobody's even looking at it."

"People around here see the river all the time." Honey glances toward the bridge's railing. "Plus, it's not like Huck and Jim are down there on a raft."

If the Mississippi River cut through the middle of Allentown, I hope I'd notice it every day. On the other hand, the Lehigh River is just a few blocks from my house, and I've never spent much time staring at that water.

Beside me, Gram stirs. She wipes an arm across her face. "Honey can drive," she mumbles, then slumps forward and snores some more. Meanwhile, Kermit's got his head shoved between me and the donut box from this morning. I grab the carton and discover one last chocolate-sprinkled. "Want to split a donut?" I ask Honey.

"Sure." She takes the half I offer and shoves the whole thing into her mouth. "Not bad."

"Mr. Kruller's are better."

"Mr. Kruller?" Honey asks me.

"He makes the best donuts in Allentown. He's also Abbey's boss."

Honey laughs. "With a name like Kruller, it would be a shame if his donuts weren't the best."

Ahead, the highway sweeps into a big left-hand curve until the sun shines directly into our faces. Honey pulls a pair of sunglasses out of her pocket and slips them on. With the dark lenses across her eyes and the tattoos stretching up her arms and across the back of her neck, she looks like some kind of comic-book action hero.

"What's it like in the Philippines?" I ask her.

She shrugs. "I've never been. I was born and raised in Nebraska."

"Like Superman," I say.

"Superman is from Kansas. Or maybe Iowa. Or maybe Maryland. It depends who you ask."

"I thought he was from Nebraska."

"Actually," says Honey, "Superman is from Krypton. That was his home planet. It exploded as a result of a nuclear chain reaction caused by an unstable radioactive core."

"You really are a geek, aren't you?"

She grins. "I've got the dinosaur tattoo to prove it."

The Mississippi River is behind us now, and we're rolling into Iowa. Honey tells me about growing up in the Midwest, about fixing cars with her dad, who is a mechanic, and about falling in love with paleontology. "It all started with Peter Rabbit," she explains.

I gave her a blank look.

"You've never heard of Peter Rabbit?"

I shake my head.

"How about Miss Moppet? Tom Kitten? Jemima Puddle-Duck? Squirrel Nutkin?"

"Are you making this up?"

"I'm totally serious. There's also Johnny Town-Mouse, Timmy Tiptoes, and don't forget Squirrel Nutkin's little brother, Twinkleberry."

"No," I say, "we can't forget about Twinkleberry."

"When I was little," Honey explains, "I was deeply obsessed with Beatrix Potter books."

"Beatrix Potter? Like Harry Potter?"

"Beatrix Potter is much better," Honey tells me. "She's real. She wrote and illustrated all the Peter Rabbit books and all the stories about his friends and family too. I loved those books, and when I got older, I wanted to know everything about her. I discovered that she was this really remarkable woman. She was an artist and a writer, and she was also a historian, conservationist, scientist, botanist, sheep breeder, and I'm sure I'm leaving a dozen things out. She was amazing. She used to keep pet rabbits," Honey continues, "and when they died, she boiled them down until there was nothing left but the skull and bones."

"Wait a minute," I say. "She boiled her own bunnies?"

"She wanted to see how all the bones fit together and how the joints worked. She was just really curious. She boiled birds and mice and other animals too. From there, she could figure out how they moved, which made it possible to draw them as realistically as possible."

"She boiled them?" I say again.

"Don't worry," Honey says. "They were already dead."

"How does this get you to dinosaurs?"

"I used to hike around the fields and parks near my house. Sometimes I found dead animals out there, and when I read what Beatrix Potter did, I went ahead and boiled my dead animals too. And you know what?"

"What?" I ask.

"It was cool! You really can see how all the bones work!"

By now, my grandmother is awake and rubbing her eyes.

"To tell you the truth," says Honey, "I didn't really boil the dead animals at first. I put them in our dishwasher and ran them through the extra-high-heat pot-scrubbing cycle. That scoured the flesh right off."

Gram turns toward me. "What in the world are you two talking about?"

"How to strip the flesh off Squirrel Nutkin," I tell her.

"What about Twinkleberry?" Gram says.

Honey laughs. "I'm explaining how I fell in love with bones."

"Got it," says Gram.

"When we get to your house," I say to Honey, "please remind me to not eat off of any plates that come out of your dishwasher."

Abbey stretches, sits up straight, and looks out the window. "Are we there yet?"

"Not yet," says Honey.

"How far are we from Utah?"

"Around a thousand miles," Honey tells her.

Abbey rubs her eyes. "How far are we from Allentown?"

"Around a thousand miles," Gram offers.

"Halfway there!" says Abbey.

I reach into the backpack at my feet, grab the binoculars, and use them to look out the rearview window. I feel carsick almost immediately. Perhaps it has something to do with staring at the world through dual magnifying glasses while facing backward at highway speeds. Still, I continue to gaze east. I imagine our big yellow Buick moving like a tiny toy car across a giant tabletop road map. I see us rolling from Pennsylvania to Chicago and across the Mighty Mississippi. I wonder what it will be like when we get to the Great Plains and the Rocky Mountains and the Utah desert.

"Can you see home?" Abbey asks me.

I shake my head.

"We've come too far to look back now," says Gram.

I lower the binoculars. Happily, the carsick feeling goes away almost immediately. At the same time, I'm sort of overwhelmed at the distance we've already traveled.

And we still have a long way to go.

Chapter Seven

The Miracle of the Loaves and Creamy Peanut Butter

I DON'T REMEMBER much about Iowa. Mostly, I doze on and off and have weird dreams about dinosaurs chasing me across huge, wide cornfields. I guess I cry out in my sleep because Gram grabs my arm and shakes me awake. "Leo," she says. "Leo, it's just a dream. Wake up."

"Don't eat me!" I holler. I leap back and smack my head on the window, which makes my eyes pop open.

Abbey turns to face me in the backseat. "That must have hurt."

"It did."

"What's eating you?" Gram asks.

I blink and try to remember. "Velociraptors."

Abbey laughs. "I don't think so."

"How would you know?"

"What did they look like?"

"Claws. Teeth. Two legs. Tail." I curl my fingers and wave my arms at Abbey. "You know."

"Velociraptors are the size of chickens, Leo."

"These were bigger than chickens."

"Probably *deinonychus*," offers Honey.

Abbey nods. "That's what I was going to say."

Gram reaches over and pulls me closer to her side. "It was a dream, Leo. You're all right now." I lean against my grandmother. I guess she's not mad at me anymore, and that feels good. "Sometimes," Gram tells me, "dreams are where we do our best thinking."

"This was more of a nightmare."

"A nightmare convinced me to marry your grandfather."

"Oh?" says Abbey.

"He proposed," Gram says. "I said no. Then I went home, I went to bed, and I dreamt that he died."

"Whoa," says Abbey.

"How did he die?" asks Honey. "I mean in your dream."

"I killed him," says Gram.

"Whoa!" Abbey says again.

"He was about to marry some other girl, and that just wasn't going to work for me."

"So you killed him?" my cousin asks.

"You're missing the point," says Gram.

"Which is?"

"She couldn't live without him," says Honey.

Gram nods. "Exactly."

"That is very romantic," says Abbey, "in a very weird way."

I shake my head. "Killing somebody in your dreams is not romantic."

Gram laughs. "It's better than being eaten by chickenosaurs."

Honey glances at Gram in the rearview mirror. "Did you ever tell your husband about that dream?"

"I did," says Gram. "We were married forty-six years, and he never looked at another woman."

"No surprise there," says Abbey.

Outside, the sun has set just below the horizon. We're on a simple two-lane road rolling past cornfields that stretch as far as I can see. It's still light out, but it won't be for long. Even now, a sliver of moon is following us low in the sky. "Where are we?" I ask.

"Nebraska City," says Honey.

I look outside again. There's still nothing but corn. "This is Nebraska City?"

"This isn't the city part."

Just then, the Buick's engine coughs and shudders.

"We can't be out of gas," says Gram. "We filled the tank less than an hour ago."

The car shudders again.

"My dad will check it out when we get home," Honey promises. "He's a mechanic," she reminds us, "and we're almost there."

A few moments later, Honey brings us into downtown Nebraska City. Around us, low-slung brick-and-stone storefronts look like little boxes lined up on a model train set. Everything is so neat and clean. And unlike Pennsylvania, it seems like there's nothing behind these buildings but sky. If I stood on one of the roofs,

I bet the horizon would look a thousand miles away. I guess Gram was right when she said that the universe stretches beyond Allentown.

We pass a small park, then drive by a couple shops, a corner café, and the Nebraska City Middle School. Honey points toward the school playground. "That's where I got my first kiss and my first bloody nose."

"I hope it wasn't on the same day," says Abbey.

Honey laughs. "As a matter of fact, it was."

We cross a bumpy set of Nebraska City railroad tracks and turn into a residential neighborhood where every yard has a fat green tree near a front stoop that holds a watering can or a wooden bucket filled with flowers. Honey swings the Buick onto a gravel lane, then drives onto a wide grassy yard set between a big blue house and an old red barn. A light on the barn sheds a soft glow over a dozen or so cars parked nearby. Honey turns the key, and the Electra's engine goes quiet. "Welcome home," she tells us.

I point at the parked cars around us. "Do all these belong to you?"

"Some do," says Honey. "Some are for sale. The rest belong to Dad's customers."

"Who's got to pee?" Gram asks.

"Pick me," says Abbey.

Gram opens her door. "Age before beauty."

Kermit scrambles across Gram's lap and heads into the grass before anybody else can step out of the Buick. From there, the dog quickly finds a spot to do his business. "Once again," says Gram, "the lower rungs of the animal kingdom prevail over mankind."

Honey leads us across the yard and toward the house.

"Did you let your parents know you were bringing friends home?" I ask.

Honey pushes the door open and leads us into a spacious kitchen, where we find a kind-looking, middle-aged Filipino couple seated at the table. "Mom! Dad!" says Honey. "I'm home, and I brought friends!"

Honey's parents hop to their feet. "Hello!" shouts Mr. Buenafe.

"Welcome!" adds his wife.

Honey turns to me and grins. "Now they know you're coming."

Mrs. Buenafe, who'd been slicing a huge loaf of bread when we came in, has a long, black-handled bread knife in her hand. She's running around with it in the air and stopping occasionally to hug everybody.

"Lily!" Mr. Buenafe yells at her. "Be careful with the knife!"

Kermit is barking, and Honey is laughing. Gram and Abbey are both shaking Mr. Buenafe's hands. I'm just trying to avoid the bread knife.

"Welcome!" Mrs. Buenafe says to me. "Welcome!" She wraps me in a hug while Mr. Buenafe reaches over the kitchen table and plucks the knife from his wife's hand. As he pulls it away, the blade nicks my ear.

I press my hand against the side of my head. "Ouch," I say in as calm a voice as possible.

"Look what you did!" Mrs. Buenafe shouts to her husband.

"You're the one waving that *kampílan* around!" he hollers back.

"*Kampílan?*" I ask.

"Big knife," explains Honey.

My palm feels wet. I move my hand away from my head. A big drop of blood splashes onto the table. "Uh-oh."

"It's just a flesh wound," Abbey assures me.

"It's only a tiny cut," Gram adds.

"It's okay," I say. "I'm okay." But suddenly, I feel dizzy. My knees get weak, and my voice sounds far away. The room begins to spin. "I don't like blood," I confess. I sit heavily on the floor while everybody starts talking to me at once.

"Look up at the ceiling."

"Put your head between your legs."

"Do you feel like you're going to pass out?"

"Put pressure on the lobe."

"There's hardly any blood," says Abbey. "Leo, don't think about the blood."

"Could you stop saying the word *blood*?" I take a deep breath and get to my feet. "I'm really okay."

Mrs. Buenafe takes my chin, then presses a dish towel against my ear. "I'd hate to see you when you're not okay."

A moment later, I'm in the bathroom with Gram and Mrs. Buenafe, who are trying to dab dark stains off my shirt. "You'll have to take it off," Mrs. Buenafe tells me.

I do as I'm told, and she takes the shirt away.

"Sorry," I tell Gram, who keeps an arm on my elbow in case I decide to pass out.

"There's no need to be sorry." Gram pulls the towel away from my head and presses a Band-Aid against my ear. "Nothing brings people together like a crisis."

"I'm glad I could help." I glance down at my bare chest. "I have to get a new shirt."

Just then, the door swings open. Honey and Abbey join us in the bathroom. "Are you going to live?" Abbey asks.

I cross my arms across my chest. "Do you know how to knock?"

"Wow," Honey says to me. "You're skinny."

"How would you like it if I said that to you when your shirt was off?"

"That's not going to happen." Honey hands me a dark blue T-shirt. "This is for you."

I take the tee and hold it up. The front features a cartoon red tow truck beneath a golden yellow sun. The back says, HAVE FAITH IN BUENAFE.

Abbey nods at the words. "Very funny."

Gram and Honey smile, but I don't get the joke.

"*Buena*," says Abbey. "And *Fe*. In Spanish, that means 'good faith.'" She points at the T-shirt. "Have faith in good faith."

"When did you learn Spanish?" I ask.

She shrugs. "I watch *Betty, La Fea* on YouTube."

I pull the shirt over my head. It's huge, but at least it's blood-free. I strike a body builder's pose and turn to Honey and Abbey. "Feast your eyes on *Leo, la fea!*" I have no idea what I just said, but it makes everybody laugh.

"I don't think so," Honey tells me.

Gram pats me on the back. "You're more handsome than ever, Leo."

Together, we make our way back to the kitchen, where we all take a seat. Kermit's already beneath the table, curled up and fast asleep as if he's right at home. "Didn't he get enough sleep in the car?" I ask.

"Kermit is an old dog," Abbey reminds me.

"I know how he feels," says Gram. She looks really tired too.

Meanwhile, Mrs. Buenafe places bread and fruit plus peanut butter and jelly on the kitchen table. There are sliced vegetables and potato chips and cookies too. "It's the miracle of the loaves and creamy peanut butter," she announces.

A few minute later, everybody is talking and eating as if we've known one another forever. Mr. Buenafe is asking Gram and me about the Buick. Mrs. Buenafe is preparing a bowl of vanilla ice cream for Kermit. Honey is trying to convince Abbey to enroll at the University of Nebraska one day. Mr. Buenafe stops and points at my Band-Aid, which makes me feel like I've got an elephant ear stuck to the side of my head. "Now you know what it's like to be married to Mrs. Buenafe."

Mrs. Buenafe laughs, then yells at her husband. "You are a very lucky man."

"It's true," Mr. Buenafe admits. "I am a very lucky man." He leans toward me and speaks in a loud whisper. "Just the same, families are a risky business."

"I know all about that," I tell him.

Gram reaches across the table and whacks me on the back of the head. "Leo," she says, "don't be like your mother."

I rub my head. "What's that supposed to mean?"

"If you focus only on the risks, then you don't get the rewards."

Looking around the Buenafe's kitchen, which is filled with laughter and fun and food and talk, I have to admit that maybe my grandmother is right.

Chapter Eight

Carburetors, Champorado, and Dinosaur Bones

I WAKE UP THE NEXT MORNING with a green sofa pillow over my head and a red, white, and blue afghan wrapped around my legs. I'm in a small living room with a woven oval carpet on the floor, hundreds and hundreds of books stacked on shelves along the walls, and just as many framed family photos everywhere else. Somebody must have carried me in here last night, but I don't remember any of it.

I untangle myself from the blanket, sit up, and open the curtains that cover a window behind the couch where I was sleeping. Outside, Gram and Abbey stand next to our Buick. The hood is open, and Honey's father is leaning over the fender to check the engine. Honey sits behind the steering wheel. "Hit it!" Mr. Buenafe shouts at her.

Honey presses the gas pedal. The engine roars. *RAAAAAWWWWRRR!* Then it backfires. *BOOM! BOOM! BOOM!*

Mr. Buenafe reaches under the hood with a wrench and gives something a turn. The car settles into a steadier rumble. "Got it!" he shouts.

I turn away from the window, then make my way to the kitchen, where Honey's mom sits at the table with a laptop and a stack of auto parts catalogs. "Good morning," I say.

Mrs. Buenafe looks up. "It's morning in Manila. It's afternoon in Nebraska City."

I glance at a wall clock that's shaped like a black plastic cat with a tail for a pendulum. It's half past one. "Sorry."

"I'm the one who should be apologizing to you. You were barely inside my house, and I tried to cut your ears off."

"I'm all healed," I promise.

Mrs. Buenafe stands and examines both sides of my head. "No blood. That's good. Are you hungry?"

My stomach growls loudly.

Mrs. Buenafe laughs, then heads for a kitchen cabinet. I pull out a chair and discover Kermit still sleeping beneath the table. I reach down and rub behind his ears. "Good morning," I whisper.

Kermit opens one eye, thumps his tail three times on the floor, stretches his paws, and falls back asleep.

I flip through a parts catalog while Mrs. Buenafe places an old black pot atop a white, gas stove. She pours ingredients into the pot, then gives it a stir. "Your grandmother says you helped rebuild that Buick."

I nod.

"Then you know that a car from 1973 was not designed to survive in the twenty-first century. Your carburetor is dying."

I remember Pop saying something about the Buick's carburetor when we put the car back together. "It's from the gas," I recall now. "It's running rough because we use different gasoline today than they used back then."

"Gas has changed. Cars have changed. Everything's

changed." Mrs. Buenafe continues stirring the stove-top pot. "Cars don't even have carburetors anymore."

"My grandfather said we should pour in an additive every time we fill the gas tank, especially if we ever decided to take it on a long trip."

"Your grandfather was right."

"I forgot."

"It's not a crisis. The carb's not dead yet. But if you replace it now and remember the additive, your car will be good as new."

"How much is a carburetor?" I ask.

"You brought Honey home. You're family now. No charge for you."

"You don't charge your family?"

"We don't have a lot of family around here." Mrs. Buenafe puts a bowl with something brown and white and sweet smelling in front of me. She hands me a spoon. "This is champorado. Eat."

I stare at the dish. It doesn't look like anything I've ever had before.

"Blow on it," adds Mrs. Buenafe. "It's hot."

I do as I'm told, then take a tiny bite.

"So?" she asks.

I don't know what I'm expecting, but what I get is a surprise. "It's chocolate!"

Mrs. Buenafe smiles. "It's champorado."

I take a bigger bite. "It's a bowl of chocolate!"

Mrs. Buenafe nods. "Traditional Filipino breakfast."

Just then, the screen door swings open, and we're joined in the kitchen by Honey, Abbey, and Mr. Buenafe. "We've got bad news, good news, bad news, and good news," my cousin tells me.

"I know about the carburetor," I say through a mouthful of chocolate-rice-pudding stuff.

"That's the bad news. The good news is that we can fix it, and it won't cost anything."

I look toward Mr. Buenafe. "Thank you."

"No problem," he tells me, "but I have to get the parts."

"That's the bad news," says Abbey. "It will take three or four days to get what we need."

I look up from my bowl.

"But don't worry," she says before I can speak. "The good news is that we can still leave today."

"How?" I ask.

"Francine bought a car. Actually, it's a pine-green Jeep, which is much more appropriate for dinosaur hunting than an old Buick Electra, don't you think?" Abbey doesn't wait for me to answer. "She's test-driving it now. Mr. Buenafe wants to give it to us like a loaner, but your grandmother insists on paying for it."

"Come back after you visit Utah," Mr. Buenafe tells us. "I'll have your Buick fixed, and I'll buy the Jeep back from you if you'd like." He grins. "It's a money-back guarantee."

"Where's Gram now?" I ask.

"She went to the store," Abbey tells me. "She said she'd be right back."

"The Jeep is good," Mr. Buenafe promises.

"Good enough to go dinosaur hunting?" Honey asks her father.

Mr. Buenafe grins. "No problem."

Honey turns to the kitchen counter and retrieves an old cardboard box stuffed with guidebooks and road atlases. "Your grandmother told me you're heading to the Cleveland-Lloyd Dinosaur Quarry."

I take another bite of champorado. "We're going to see the allosaurs."

"Right," says Honey. "But she says it's in Price, Utah, and that's not exactly true." Honey pulls a frayed gas station map of Utah out of the box and spreads it across the kitchen table. She points to a spot sort of near the center of the state. "Price is here." She drags her finger south for a couple inches. "The Cleveland-Lloyd quarry is closer to here."

"That doesn't seem too far," says Abbey.

"That's an hour of driving through the middle of nowhere," Honey warns her. "NASA tested the Mars rovers in the desert out there. I think they filmed Star Trek alien landscapes out that way too."

"Are there roads?" I ask.

"They're mostly dirt roads. They're good enough, but you have to be careful."

Mr. Buenafe steps forward and studies the map. He points at a spot in the far northeast corner of Utah. "Why not visit Dinosaur National Monument? We've been camping there. It's very beautiful, very interesting, and it's a much easier drive than the one you're talking about."

I shake my head. "It's got to be allosaurs."

Abbey glances at the tiny dinosaur tattoo on Honey's wrist. "It's the Different Lizard."

Honey gives my cousin a smile. "That makes sense to me."

"Not to me," says Mr. Buenafe, "but you're the ones doing the driving."

I recall Gram telling us how thousands and thousands of allosaur bones had been uncovered at the Cleveland-Lloyd Dinosaur Quarry. "Are we really going to see big piles of allosaur bones?" I ask Honey.

Honey shakes her head. "Mostly you're going to see a hole in the ground. Dinosaur quarries look more like shallow graves than *Jurassic Park*, Leo. But they're where you dig up clues that get pieced together into stories about the world."

Abbey pushes wavy brown hair away from her face. "That sounds awesome."

Honey folds the Utah road map and hands it to my cousin. "It is pretty awesome. It can also be very frustrating. The clues are really old, you rarely have them all, and you don't necessarily understand the ones you've got. Also, every time you get a new clue, it might be time to throw away everything you thought you already knew."

I recall something Pop used to say to his students. "Scientists, journalists, novelists, and historians all have the same job. They make up stories, figure out which ones are most likely to be true, then go back and do it again."

Honey nods. "That's exactly right."

"So science is just making up stories?"

"Science is making up true stories," Honey tells me.

"That's what I want to do," says Abbey.

Honey gives her a big grin. "When you come back, you really should sit in on a couple of my classes at the university."

The thought of coming back makes me wonder when we are going to leave. I glance at the black-and-white cat clock on the wall. I don't know exactly when Gram pulled away in the Jeep, but I'm guessing it's been at least half an hour since she headed out for her test-drive. "Gram should have been back by now."

"She is taking a long time," Abbey agrees.

Suddenly, I feel panic rising in my chest. "Did she take anything with her?"

"Just her keys," says Mrs. Buenafe.

"Why did she need her keys to test-drive the Jeep?" Before anyone can answer, I rush outside. Abbey follows along with Honey and her parents. We find the trunk of the Electra unlatched. Kermit's dog food is still in there. Gram's bags are gone.

"Tell me that she did not head to Utah without us," Abbey says.

I don't respond.

Abbey glances between the trunk and me. "Did she really leave?"

I take a big breath. I should have been keeping an eye on Gram. I know she likes to wander away. But between sleeping past noon, stuffing my face with chocolate champorado, and chatting about road maps and dinosaur bones, I let my attention wander.

"She probably left the trunk open so you could get to Kermit's dog food," says Honey.

Abbey puts her hands on her hips. "That means this was premeditated. Not to mention she took the car keys."

"That doesn't matter," I say.

"Of course it matters!" shouts Abbey.

I reach behind the Buick's rear license plate and remove a little magnetic box that holds the set of spare keys that Pop and I hid back there over a year ago. I toss the keys to Abbey. "It really doesn't matter. What matters is that Gram's got her own Jeep, the open road, and nobody with her." I take another breath, then let the air out of my lungs slowly. "This is my fault."

Mrs. Buenafe puts her hands on her hips. "Your grandmother just left you in Nebraska with strangers. How exactly is that your fault?"

I think about it for a moment. "Okay," I finally admit. "This isn't my fault, but—"

"But what?"

"You don't feel like strangers."

Mrs. Buenafe's expression softens. Even Abbey calms down a little. "Leo's right about that," my cousin tells Honey's family. Then she turns to me. "So now what?"

"Do you want to skip the dinosaur quarry?"

Abbey's eyes go wide and her mouth drops open. "Have you lost your mind?"

"Then it's settled." I turn to Honey and her parents, and I say what needs to be said. "Abbey and I have got to go."

Chapter Nine

Haw Haws, Pusit, and Other Things That Matter

MR. AND MRS. BUENAFE lean into the Buick through the driver's side window. "You definitely know where you're going?" Mrs. Buenafe asks Abbey and me.

"Cleveland-Lloyd Dinosaur Quarry," I say.

"And you're sure you know the way?"

Abbey holds up her phone, which shows a map. I pat the collection of atlases and travel guides the Buenafes have given us. They're stacked in a pile on the Buick's front seat and basically cover every square mile between New Orleans, Winnipeg, Anchorage, and the Hawaiian Islands. "We'll find it," I promise.

Abbey places her phone on the seat between us. "And we'll bring back the Jeep."

"Don't worry about the Jeep," says Mr. Buenafe. "And don't forget to use that fuel additive I gave you." While we were packing, he put a whole bunch of little bottles labeled DOCTOR JOHN'S LIQUID CARB DOCTOR into our trunk. We're supposed to pour one bottle into the Buick's tank every time we stop for gas. "It might run a little rough," he adds, "but your carburetor still works well enough, and this old car still has a lot of miles left in her."

Abbey starts the engine. It's her unsubtle way of telling everybody that she really wants to get moving. Mr. and Mrs. Buenafe step away.

"Don't drive for too long at a stretch," Mrs. Buenafe tells us. "And be sure to eat and drink." That won't be a problem because in addition to Doctor John's Liquid Carb Doctor, the Buenafes put a huge box of snacks along with several cases of bottled water on the back-seat next to Kermit.

I look up at Honey, who's standing next to my passenger-side window. "You have a really nice mom."

Honey grins. "I told her you liked snacks."

"Remember," Mr. Buenafe says in an I'm-giving-you-important-information-now voice, "this isn't going to be like driving around Chicago. Once you get to Utah, it's desert and mountains and canyons out there. You might go a hundred miles without seeing another car, so be careful."

"We will," Abbey promises.

"And don't forget to look around," Honey adds. "You're driving across America. Don't miss it."

"We won't," I say.

"And don't run out of gas," says Mrs. Buenafe. "And don't break down."

"You better go," Honey tells us, "or my parents will end up coming with you."

Abbey takes her foot off the brake pedal, and we begin to roll away. "Good-bye!" she and I yell to the Buenafes. "We'll see you soon!"

Abbey steers out of the driveway, then takes us back toward Nebraska City. Soon we turn onto a two-lane highway and head west. With our windows rolled down, the smell of cow manure drifts through the car from surrounding farms. I never thought I'd say this, but the cow smell is kind of nice. I turn toward my cousin. "You know the date, right?"

Abbey nods. "August 29. Your grandfather died exactly one year ago today."

"If Gram was going to lose her mind, then this was the day she was going to do it."

"She didn't lose her mind, Leo."

"How do you know?"

Abbey reaches into a pocket and pulls out a crumpled piece of paper. "I found this on the dashboard."

I take the paper, which waves and flaps in the breeze that's blasting through the car. It's easy to recognize Gram's familiar handwriting. "'I haven't lost my mind,'" I read out loud. "'Wait for me in Nebraska with Honey's family. They're good people. I'll be back in a couple days, and we'll drive back to Pennsylvania together.'" I turn to my cousin. "What was she thinking?"

Abbey shakes her head. "Maybe she is crazy. I mean, first I had to miss the Field Museum. Now she thinks I'm going to miss a real dinosaur quarry? That's not going to happen."

"Can we catch her?" I ask.

Abbey glances at her phone. "According to this, we've got about fourteen hours of driving between here and the dinosaur quarry. Francine's got at least a one-hour head start. Algebra says that there's no way we can catch up with her today."

"Who put algebra in charge?"

"Do the math," Abbey tells me. "If she's sixty miles ahead and traveling down the highway at her regular speed—"

"Which is about eighty miles an hour."

"We'd have to average a hundred miles an hour in order to see her before suppertime. I don't think that's a good idea. Plus, I don't think Francine wants us to catch her. She wants to be alone. We should respect that, Leo."

"But we are going to catch her?" I ask.

Abbey nods. "We'll catch her."

"And then we can kill her?"

"Definitely." Abbey rummages beneath the maps between us. She finds her cell phone, then shoves it at me. "In the meantime, you have to call your mother."

I don't take the phone. "Now you're the one that's acting crazy."

"Leo," says Abbey, "I understand if Francine wants

to make the last part of this trip by herself. But that doesn't mean she isn't depressed or manic or insane or worse. We have to tell your mom."

I sigh. What if my grandmother really is losing her marbles? What if she has some kind of disease that she's been keeping a secret? Mom's mentioned Alzheimer's and depression and dementia, but I never believed any of it. Of course, what do I know? I'm a kid. And disease is not something you believe or disbelieve. Diseases are true or not true. But when it comes to my family, who knows what's true?

"Do you know about Peter?" I ask my cousin now.

"Who's Peter?"

"Mom had a younger brother named Peter. He got hit by a car when he was little. He died. Mom and Pop would never let anybody talk about it."

"Why not?" Abbey asks.

I shrug. "It was like a rule. Gram told me about him for the first time yesterday."

Abbey keeps her eyes on the road. "I guess the rules are changing, Leo."

"Maybe that's why we're riding down a highway in the middle of Nebraska right now," I suggest.

"Maybe." Abbey pushes the phone toward me again. "Phone home, Leo."

"This is not going to be good," I warn her.

"It won't be that bad. I called your mother when we were in Chicago. She knows we're all right."

I remember Abbey shoving the phone into her pocket when I found her on the museum steps. "We're not all right anymore."

"That's why you need to call her."

I take the phone and dial. Mom picks up on the first ring. "Mom?" I say.

"Leo!" she hollers. "Stay right where you are! I'm coming to get you!"

"Mom—"

"Put your grandmother on the phone."

"But—"

"Just put her on the phone."

"I can't."

"Why not?"

"She's not here anymore." There is a long silence. I'm not used to that from my mother. "Mom?"

"Where is she?" Mom asks quickly.

I have no idea where to even begin, so I say nothing.

"Is she . . ."

"Is she what?" I ask.

"Dead?"

"Of course not!" I holler. "Mom, here's the thing . . ."

While Abbey and I roll past huge fields of corn, I explain the whole situation. I tell Mom about Chicago and the tow truck and the Buenafes and everything. I also remind her that today is the anniversary of Pop's death.

"I know what day it is," Mom tells me.

"We have to catch Gram," I say. "But we can't do it today, and we can't—"

"Leo—" Mom says.

"And please don't say she's crazy." I feel myself getting upset as I recall how hurt Gram looked when she learned what I told the cop about her back in Chicago. "She's not crazy. She's just—"

"Leo," Mom says again.

"She's in a big green Jeep, so she should be easy to find. I'm really sorry. We just have to—"

"LEO!" Mom shouts.

I stop. "What?"

"Where are you now?"

I catch my breath and look outside. There's nothing but corn and clouds and blue sky as far as I can see. "We're in Nebraska, but we're heading to the Cleveland-Lloyd Dinosaur Quarry. That's in Utah. We'll get there tomor—"

"I'll meet you there," Mom says.

I stop. "You'll what?"

"I'll meet you there," Mom says again. "I'm on my way."

All of a sudden, I can't speak.

"Leo," Mom says. "Are you all right?"

I hesitate and then tell Mom the truth. "I'm all right. I miss you."

There's a pause, and then Mom replies, "I miss you too."

"We're really having an adventure."

"We sure are," Mom says quietly.

"Cleveland-Lloyd Dinosaur Quarry," I tell her again. "It's near a town called Price."

"I'll find you," she promises.

I lower the phone when I'm sure that Mom is no longer on the line. "She's going to meet us in Utah." I tell Abbey.

My cousin nods. "Good job, Leo."

We ride in silence for a few miles until Abbey glances over her shoulder toward the backseat. "Do you think there's any chocolate in that snack box?"

I turn around and pop open the carton that's next to Kermit. The big dog gets to his feet and sticks his head into the box to check things out for himself.

"What have we got?" asks Abbey.

I fold back the flap. "There's apples, water bottles, a box of graham crackers, and a whole bunch of things I've never heard of before." I grab several small neon-colored snack bags and show them to Abbey. "Would you like Boy Bawang Bar-B-Q Flavor Cornick? Teriyaki Style Crispy Pusit? Nagaraya Hot & Spicy Cracker Nuts? Captain Sid's Butong Pakwan? Or Haw Haw Milk Powder Candy?"

"No Hershey bars?"

"Haw Haws, yes. Hershey's, no." According to the labels, all these snack foods are made in the Philippines. I think back to Honey's tattoos and the chocolate champorado. Nebraska City is definitely the Buenafes' home, but they've stayed connected with their past too.

I wonder if there are any secret dead uncles or runaway grandmas buried in the Buenafe family history.

"In that case," says Abbey, "pass the Pusit."

"Are you sure?" I examine the Teriyaki Style Crispy Pusit label. "It's definitely not chocolate."

"If you can't get what you want, then try something totally different." Abbey takes the bag and rips it open. "That's my life philosophy."

"I didn't know you had a life philosophy."

"I didn't until just now." She reaches into the package, pulls out a strange-looking object, and quickly pops it into her mouth. That's when the smell reaches me. It is not a smell that I like.

I look more closely at the snack bag. "You realize you're eating squid?"

"Leo," Abbey says, "it might be time to change my life philosophy." She pulls the car to the shoulder, leaps out, and begins spitting half-chewed Crispy Pusit onto the ground.

"Are you all right?" I call after her.

"Water!" she cries. "Hurry!"

I grab a bottle from the backseat, then run it over to my cousin, who's wiping her tongue with her sleeve.

"That was not enjoyable," she reports as if I couldn't tell for myself.

Kermit, who's stepped out of the car, examines the Pusit bag Abbey threw in the dirt. The dog sniffs at it once, then jumps back as if he's been bitten.

"It's probably an acquired taste," I suggest. "How about some Cornick or a cracker nut?"

Abbey is too busy pouring water down her throat to answer. "Hot!" she gargles. "Really hot!"

I hand her an apple, which she bites and then uses to dab at her mouth like a sponge. "Okay," Abbey says after a little while, "I think I can drive now."

"Was it that bad?"

"Try it," Abbey suggests.

"Trying things is your life philosophy. Not mine."

That makes Abbey laugh. "What's your life philosophy, Leo?"

"I haven't figured it out yet."

Abbey considers this. "'I haven't figured it out yet' is not a bad life philosophy."

Back in the Buick, Abbey pulls onto the highway while I fuss with the radio. We settle on a station that apparently plays all Elvis all the time. While we sing along with the King, Abbey and I play the cloud-shape game. "I see a dragon," I say.

"I think it's a *Parasaurolophus*," Abbey tells me.

"What's wrong with dragons?"

"It's more fun to say *Parasaurolophus*."

As the day moves toward evening, the clouds lose their shapes until they look like long, rolling carpets in the sky. We stop for gas, take Kermit for a walk, and remember to pour Doctor John's Liquid Carb Doctor into the Buick. Later, we even go back to the snack box, where we learn that Captain Sid's Butong Pakwan are tasty salted watermelon seeds, Haw Haw Milk Powder Candy reminds us of Necco Wafers, Boy Bawang Bar-B-Q Flavor Cornick tastes more like garlic than anything else, and Nagaraya Hot & Spicy Cracker Nuts are actually peanuts baked inside cracker shells. The cracker nuts are seasoned with a set of spices that seem specially made to incinerate the inside of your mouth.

"The good news," says Abbey after we finish the Cracker Nuts, "is that I can't taste the Pusit anymore. The bad news is that I can't taste anything anymore."

I point at a highway sign on the side of the road.

"The other good news is that Colorado is less than a hundred miles away. Do you want to take a rest soon?"

Abbey shakes her head. "I've still got a lot of driving left in me. We don't want to keep the allosaurs waiting."

"They've been waiting for millions of years," I remind her. "A few more won't kill them."

"Especially since they're already dead."

"There's that," I confirm.

"Do you think anybody will be talking about us in a million years, Leo?"

"A million years is a long time," I say as we roll across the dusky desert plain of western Nebraska.

Abbey nods. "By then, it will be nothing but robots and cockroaches just sitting around talking about the good old days."

Abbey is right. Millions of years from now, everybody and everything I know will be gone. Nobody will be talking about us. Nobody will care. Nobody will know about Buick Electras or Haw Haw Milk Powder Candy or Elvis Presley or anything at all. In the future, none of this will matter.

But you know what? It matters now.

Chapter Ten

An Important Fact About Bears

THE SETTING SUN BARELY tops the western horizon when we pass a sign that says WELCOME TO COLORFUL COLORADO.

Despite the enthusiastic slogan, the early evening light reveals miles and miles of flat brown land around us. Meanwhile, huge splashes of red and gold and dusky green pour across the white clouds above. "I hope Gram is seeing this," I tell Abbey, who leans forward to admire the sky.

"I know," she whispers.

Soon, night catches up with us, and stars begin to appear. Eventually, their twinkling is overwhelmed by a different light. It's the electric glow from Denver, which is a much bigger city than I expected. On the highway, we pass endless grids filled with neighborhoods and office buildings and even an old amusement park. Abbey turns my way. "Do you think your grandmother will get that dinosaur tattoo?"

"I have no idea," I admit.

"If she does, then she's probably stopped in Denver for the night. I bet we're driving past her right now."

I look outside. Around us, traffic has slowed to a crawl while we inch past a brightly lit construction site. Just a few feet away, workers in neon-orange vests wield jackhammers and power tools. The noise makes my teeth vibrate. After the long, quiet stretches of road we've been on all day, I am not enjoying the city. "I don't see any tattoo parlors," I tell Abbey. "Let's keep going."

"That works for me."

It takes a while, but we finally put the construction zone and most of the city behind us. "Are we in the Rocky Mountains?" I ask.

"I think so," Abbey says. We both peer out our windows, but it's too dark to really see anything except more highway and an occasional billboard. I notice a roadside sign that appears to show a life-size red, white, and blue stegosaur sculpture wearing a snazzy vest and a tall top hat. "What do you think that's about?"

"The latest in Jurassic style?" Abbey suggests.

"It looks Cretaceous to me."

Abbey shakes her head. "I hate it when people mix up their dinosaur fashions."

Soon, the lights of Denver are long gone, and it's clear that we're heading uphill. Not only that, it's noticeably cooler. We drive past places with names like Idaho Springs and Silverthorne and Frisco. I point out a sign that says OFFICERS GULCH. "It even sounds like the Wild West. YIPPEE-KI-YAY!" I yell.

Abbey rubs her eyes. "Listen, cowboy. Is it all right if we get off at the next exit? I'm exhausted."

"Sure," I tell her, "but I didn't see any hotel signs."

"We can sleep in the car if we have to."

"Is that safe?" I ask.

"Don't worry." Abbey nods at Kermit in the back-seat. "We've got a bodyguard."

"Our bodyguard is a senior citizen who sleeps most of the time."

"But he sleeps with one eye open," Abbey tells me.

"So he's old, comatose, and half-blind. I feel a lot safer now."

"We're in the middle of nowhere," Abbey points out. "Nothing is going to happen."

The ramp for Officers Gulch appears, and Abbey turns onto a dark stretch of road, which we follow for about a mile. It ends in a dirt parking lot beside a quiet lake. There are a couple portable toilets, a simple picnic area, and pretty much nothing else. After a quick walk for Kermit and bathroom breaks for Abbey and me, we take a moment to lean against the back of the Buick and stare at the sky.

"Look at all the stars," says Abbey. "This is amazing."

In the cool mountain air, the night sky shines with more celestial light than I've ever seen before. Constellations and planets and the long silvery path of our own Milky Way galaxy glimmer and twinkle off the surface of the nearby lake. I sprint to the side of the car, reach into the backseat, and retrieve Pop's binoculars. At the back bumper, I press them into Abbey's hands. "Take a look through these." I point at a bright object glowing steadily in the sky above Scorpio. "There's Saturn."

Rather than lift the glasses to her face, Abbey stares at me for a long moment.

"Aren't you going to look?" I ask.

Abbey says nothing.

"You can see Saturn's rings with those binoculars."

Abbey shakes her head, but her grin is so big that she nearly glows in the dark.

"What?" I ask.

"You're a lot like your grandfather."

Now it's my turn to say nothing.

"He loved to show off the world," Abbey continues. "He'd get so excited that sometimes I used to think that maybe he created it all himself."

Abbey's right. Pop would literally jump up and down while we studied snowflakes through a microscope or watched bats at dusk or launched thrift-store bowling balls with a homemade catapult. "He was pretty awesome," I say.

"So are you, Leo."

Again, I find myself unable to speak.

"You're welcome." Abbey lifts the binoculars and focuses on Saturn. "Wow," she says after a moment. "You know who else would love this?"

I nod and imagine what Gram's reaction might be.

"Your mother," says Abbey.

"What?"

"Your mom loves this stuff. She wanted to be an astronomer."

I turn my attention away from the universe to face my cousin. "You are making that up."

"Am not."

"She dropped out of college," I remind Abbey.

"She dropped out of college to have you. She meant to go back, but that's easier said than done."

"How do you know?" I ask.

"Your mom's always telling me stories about herself. She doesn't want me to make the same mistakes she did."

"I'm one of those mistakes," I point out.

"Your mom traded the stars for you, Leo. And she thinks you're worth all that and more."

I look up at the sky again. My eyes have adjusted to the dark, and I notice a black outline. It's a nearby peak that reaches high into the sky. We really are in the mountains.

"I'm glad Mom's coming," I tell Abbey.

"Me too." Abbey steps away from the car and rubs her hands together. "Now let's pull some blankets out of the trunk and get some sleep."

"We're really going to sleep in the car?"

Abbey pops the trunk. "You can sleep outside if you want."

"Gram never said anything about camping."

"You can add that to the list of things your grandmother didn't mention."

——

As it works out, sleeping in the Buick is easy. The car is so wide that I can almost stretch across the front seat without touching either side door. In the morning, I am rested and ready to get back on the road.

"How about a nice bag of Cornick for breakfast?" Abbey asks from the backseat.

"I'd rather start my day with a visit to the Porta-Potty." I find my sneakers, slip them onto my feet, then open the car door. Before we can stop him, Kermit leaps out of the car. He races toward the lake, where I expect he'll answer nature's call, then go for a swim.

"Kermit!" Abbey calls after him.

The big dog ignores her. Instead, he gallops toward a set of scrubby bushes. Just as he reaches them, however, one of the fat shrubs begins to rustle and shake. The movement is followed by a sound, a sort of a *rawrp!* That's when two fat bear cubs tumble into view.

"Kermit!" I yell because I have seen enough nature channel specials to know that this is not good.

"Woof!" says the dog.

Now, Abbey is out of the car and beside me. "Kermit!" she hollers. "Come back! Come here! Here, boy!"

The dog turns toward Abbey. The bear cubs, who didn't notice us at first, look our way too. One leans toward the lake as if he is going to run away. The other takes a couple cautious steps toward the car.

"Uh-oh," I say.

That's when we hear a much louder roar coming from the lake.

And then the mother bear appears.

Suddenly, I know a brand-new fact about bears. It is an important point that magazines and books and

TV documentaries do not make clear enough. Here is the lesson I've learned: In real life, bears are big.

Bears are seriously, extremely, really and truly, very, very big.

And now a very big bear is standing between Abbey, me, Kermit, and her two bear cubs.

The big bear leans back on her haunches and roars again. Actually, it's more like a scratchy honking sound this time. From the sounds of it, she is scolding the cubs. One of them responds just like any naughty toddler might do. He turns and runs away from his mother. Unfortunately, he is running straight toward Abbey and me.

"Get in the car!" I holler.

"Kermit!" Abbey screams.

"ROARRRRR!" says the big bear.

"Woof!" Kermit races after the bear, who is chasing the toddler that's trotting toward Abbey and me. From Kermit's perspective, it must look like the mother bear is preparing to attack us. Maybe she is. Maybe that's why Kermit springs forward AND LANDS ON THE MOTHER BEAR'S BACK!

"KERMIT!" Abbey hollers again.

The big bear stops. She tries to swat the dog off her shoulders, but Kermit is just out of reach. The bear squats down and rolls onto her back. Somehow, Kermit leaps away.

"*ROARRRRR!*" the bear says again.

Abbey takes a step away from the Buick. "KERMIT! COME, KERMIT! COME!"

"GET IN THE CAR!" I yell at my cousin.

"YOU GET IN THE CAR!" she yells at me.

In the meantime, the bear is more agitated than ever. But who can blame her? Just a moment ago, she was walking by the lake and minding her own bear business. Now she's dealing with a couple unruly cubs, a crazy golden retriever, and two stupid humans bickering in the woods.

"*RAWRRRRRR!*"

"AAAAAAAAH!" I scream back because it seems like the right thing to do.

"GET OVER HERE!" Abbey yells at her dog, who suddenly decides to listen.

Kermit lowers his head and launches into a full-speed

sprint toward the Buick. I open the door, and he leaps into the front seat. Abbey and I follow. The bear roars again.

"LET'S GET OUT OF HERE!" I say.

"I'M TRYING!" says Abbey, who is fumbling through her pockets. Finally, she finds the car key, slams it into the ignition, and has us speeding back toward the highway at a thousand miles an hour.

"You said you wanted adventure," I remind her.

"That's too much adventure!" she tells me.

I start to laugh. "You're not kidding!"

Now Abbey is laughing too. "Do you still have to pee?"

"I might have done that already," I admit.

"Me too!" she says.

Honestly, we're both a little hysterical right now. I put my arm around Kermit, who is on the front seat between us. The dog is still trembling. So am I.

"That was incredible," Abbey says when she catches her breath.

I just nod. There's so much adrenaline pumping through me that I can barely speak. My body must be giving off an audible hum.

"Leo," Abbey says, "one day you and I are going to be old and gray, and we are still going to be telling the story about the time we almost got eaten by a bear."

"Nobody will ever believe this."

Abbey laughs. "But it's true!"

I shake my head. Abbey's right. Believable has nothing to do with true.

Chapter Eleven

A Person Wants to Know
That There's a Person

KERMIT LIES ON THE FRONT SEAT between Abbey and me while we drive through the Rocky Mountains. Surprisingly, he doesn't want to leave the car when we stop for gas. He doesn't even get to his feet. "Is he okay?" I ask.

Abbey rubs Kermit's back, then gives him a kiss on the nose. "There's not a scratch on him. He's probably still a little stunned."

Honestly, I'm still a little stunned too. I mean, it's not like wild bears were on our list of things to do today.

Abbey rubs behind Kermit's ear. "It's okay if he wants to stay in the car."

We fill the Buick's gas tank, including a dose of carburetor medicine, then Abbey and I take turns using the restrooms. When we're both back in the car, we offer Kermit water and food, but he's not interested in either.

"You'd think that fighting a bear would increase your appetite." I lean close to the golden retriever. "Are you okay, boy?"

Kermit's head remains resting between his two big front paws.

"What's wrong?" I ask.

The dog gives a shallow, raspy cough.

"Kermit?" I say.

I get no answer. Not even a tail wag.

"Kermit?" I rub the dog's floppy ears. He does not move. "Abbey," I say, "something's wrong."

"What do you mean?"

"Something's wrong with Kermit."

Abbey puts her hand on the big dog's chest. There's still no movement. "Stay here," my cousin orders me.

Abbey hops out of the Buick and sprints toward the gas station. She returns a moment later and throws herself behind the steering wheel. "The gas guy says there's a veterinarian about a mile away."

We turn out of the parking lot, head around one corner, and accelerate up the street. I look more closely at Kermit. His eyes are closed now. "I think you should hurry," I tell my cousin.

Abbey stomps on the gas pedal. We run through a stop sign, nearly knock a bicyclist off the road, then swerve into a small parking lot beside a squat brick building decorated with a big cartoony mural of Noah's ark on its side. "How is he?" Abbey asks.

I shake my head. I don't think Kermit is breathing. "Do you know dog CPR?"

Abbey throws her door open and pushes me away. Somehow she lifts the golden retriever all by herself, then turns and sprints into the vet's office. I run after. When I get inside, two orderlies are already helping to place Kermit on a rolling stretcher. A bearded man in a white coat approaches us. "What happened?" he asks.

Tears are running down Abbey's face, so I explain. "There was a bear. It chased us. Kermit jumped on him. Actually, I think he was a she. Because of the cubs." I take a breath. "It didn't seem like anybody got hurt!"

The man looks at me as if I might be insane. I can't say that I blame him. "You're going to have to slow down."

Abbey wipes an arm across her nose. "Are you a doctor?"

The man nods. "I am."

"THEN PLEASE STOP TALKING TO US AND GO SAVE MY DOG!"

The doctor nods, backs away, then turns and rushes after Kermit's stretcher. Abbey and I find a wooden bench in the office waiting area. Once we're seated, she really starts to cry.

"Are you okay?" I ask. I know it's a stupid question, but I don't know what else to say.

Abbey finds a tissue and blows her nose. I glance around until I realize that I'm looking for Kermit to help me comfort my cousin. "Leo," she finally says, "listen closely, because I'm about to tell you something important."

"Okay."

"One day," Abbey tells me, "you are going to be sitting next to somebody you care about. Maybe it will be your wife or your mother or your girlfriend. Maybe it will be your third cousin twice removed."

"Okay," I say again.

"That person will be crying, and when that happens, do not ask if they are okay. They are not okay. If they were okay, they would not be crying."

I don't respond.

"Also," Abbey continues, "do not sit there twiddling your thumbs. Instead, you put your hand in an appropriate spot. Maybe it's on a shoulder. Maybe you hold the other person's hand. Maybe you shove your own hand in your pocket and keep it there. You're a smart boy, so you can figure it out. And then you say, 'Is there anything I can do?' Got it?"

"Ummm . . ."

"Got it?" Abbey repeats more sternly this time.

I nod.

"I don't think you do."

I put my hand on Abbey's shoulder. "Is there anything I can do?"

"No," says Abbey. "Not really."

"Is my hand in the wrong place?"

Abbey gives a sad grin. "Your hand is fine. There's just really nothing you can do."

"Then why—"

"Because a person wants to know that there's a person in the world who would do something if they could." She takes a ragged breath. "Even if they can't."

Without thinking, I reach over and take Abbey's hand. Her fingers are soft and small and surprisingly slender, but I am struck by a sudden, vivid recollection of my grandfather's hands. His were rough and calloused and strong and gentle all at the same time. And now, like Abbey, I'm crying. I'm crying because I miss my grandfather. I'm crying because Kermit is sick. I'm crying because Gram's not here. Most of all, I think I'm crying because it seems that I have absolutely no control over any of this. I mean, first I learn that bears are seriously, extremely, really and truly, very, very big. Now I see that I am seriously, extremely, really and truly, very, very small. Both lessons feel like a kick in the head.

A half hour passes. Then another. It feels like forever. Finally, the bearded doctor enters the waiting room. "I'm sorry," he says.

Abbey covers her face with her hands. I am suddenly short of breath. Because Kermit the dog is dead.

"Where is he?" asks Abbey.

The doctor leads us to a door on the opposite side of the office. He opens it and admits us into a small exam room. Kermit is stretched across a small table near the wall. The sight of him almost makes me dizzy. Abbey takes a deep breath. "Oh," she says simply.

"What happened?" I ask.

The doctor sighs. "He was a very old dog. And you said there was a bear?"

"But the bear never touched him," I explain. "Not really. Kermit jumped on the bear's back, so—"

The doctor looks shocked. "He jumped on a bear's back?"

I nod. "So it wouldn't come after Abbey and me."

"That was very brave," the doctor says. "It was also very stressful. It was probably too much for his heart."

Abbey steps forward and buries her face in Kermit's fur. I join her and put a hand on Kermit's golden coat. He still feels soft and warm and brave and good. And yet, he's still dead.

Brave, beautiful, loved, and dead. All true at the same time. It makes my head hurt.

The doctor clears his throat. "Are you okay to answer some questions?"

"We're okay." I don't know why I say that. Sometimes good manners are a curse.

"You'll have to make some decisions about the body. We'll take care of everything if you'd like to leave him here."

Abbey lifts her head. "We're not leaving him."

"Is your car the one with the Pennsylvania license plates?" the doctor asks gently.

Abbey nods. "So?"

"So you're a long way from home."

Abbey hesitates.

I do not. "We can handle it," I say.

The doctor glances between Abbey, Kermit, and me. "He's a big dog."

I step forward and slide my arms under Kermit's chest and belly. The retriever weighs nearly as much as me, but somehow I hoist him up. "He's family," I say. "He's with us." I take a few steps. My knees feel like they're about to buckle. "We'll take care of him."

With that, I stagger through the exam room door, across the waiting room, and back to the Buick.

Chapter Twelve

Nature Takes Us All Back

WE'RE BACK ON the highway for only about a minute when Abbey pulls to the side of the road. "Thank you," she says to me.

"You're welcome," I tell my cousin.

She turns and studies the big, dead dog stretched across the backseat. "I want to bury him someplace special."

"We can do that," I promise. At the same time, it strikes me that Kermit will need a grave that's nearly as long and wide and deep as my grandfather's. "We have to get shovels," I point out.

Abbey nods. "Leo," she says after a long moment, "stopping to bury Kermit will put us even farther behind Francine."

"She'll be okay," I say.

Honestly, I have no idea whether or not that's true. By now, Gram could be anywhere. Maybe she's lost in a desert canyon or sipping a cold drink by a hotel pool or getting inked in a Denver tattoo parlor. But none of that matters. We'll get only one chance to give Kermit a proper farewell.

I point at the green EXIT sign on the road ahead. It says LEADVILLE in big white letters. "Leadville sounds like an old mining town. I bet we can find shovels there."

Together, Abbey and I unfold a map of Colorado. Leadville looks to be about forty-five minutes away. Just south of that, a small road turns west into the Rockies. It goes past places with names like Twin Lakes and Star Mountain and Independence Pass.

"I like the sound of Independence Pass," Abbey tells me.

"Then it's settled. First we stop in Leadville, then we drive toward Independence Pass."

"Thank you," my cousin tells me again.

I refold the map. "Let's get started."

A moment later, we're driving south into the Colorado countryside. At first, tall evergreens and fir trees line the road, which twists and turns as we climb into higher elevations. We cross an iron trestle bridge, and my ears pop more than once. Soon, the land to our west flattens and stretches away until it hits a massive wall of Rocky Mountains in the distance. I point toward those faraway peaks. "That's where we're headed."

But first we reach Leadville, which turns out be a much prettier place than the name implies. The town is home to a redbrick hotel, an old-fashioned opera house, and the Silver Dollar Saloon. The whole place looks like an Old West diorama. We stop at the Bighorn Hardware Store, where we buy two garden spades from a silver-haired man in a white shirt, black vest, worn cowboy boots, and a bolo tie. The only thing he's missing is a sheriff's badge, a holster, and a gun. He eyes our purchase at the cash register. "I hope you're not heading for the mines."

"We just need to dig a hole," Abbey tells him.

"Those old mines are treacherous," he warns us.

"We're going to bury our dog," I explain.

The man frowns. "I've lost a few dogs in my day. I've even lost a few wives."

"We lost my grandmother," I tell him.

"It happens."

"Can you recommend a good spot?" asks Abbey.

"To bury your dog?"

Abbey nods. "We're heading into the mountains."

The old man nods thoughtfully. "Most of the wilderness around here is government land. There might be rules about burying your dog out there. I recommend locating a spot that's as out of the way as possible. You don't want a ranger or a police officer catching you in the act of digging a grave."

I guess this guy is not a sheriff after all.

"Here's the thing," he adds. "The dead don't care where you put them, so pick a spot that feels right to you. Where's the dog now?"

"In our backseat," Abbey tells him.

The man raises an eyebrow, then hands over a shovel. "You better get a move on."

"Thanks," I say.

"I'm sorry about your grandmother," he adds.

"We're going to deal with her tomorrow," Abbey tells him.

He considers this for a moment. "There are definitely rules about burying your grandmother."

"She's not dead," I say.

"In that case, even more rules apply."

Abbey swings the shovels over her shoulder. "It's okay. We're probably going to kill her when we find her."

"Good luck to both of you," says the hardware man. "And good luck to your grandmother too. It sounds like you're all going to need it."

Back in the car, Kermit looks more dead than ever. Abbey starts the Buick, then steers us away from Leadville. A few miles out of town, we turn west toward the massive range of Rocky Mountains in the distance. "We're really going over that?" Abbey asks.

On the map, the road looks like a Slinky toy that lost a fight with a pencil sharpener. It doubles back on itself again and again and again. "We're going over that," I confirm.

Abbey settles into her seat and grips the steering wheel with both hands. "Then buckle your seat belt," she tells me.

At first, the road runs long and true, but soon we hit a couple sharp zigs and zags. We pass a few log cabins plus a set of twin lakes that are almost too pretty to be real. A herd of small deer wanders along the roadside, and hawks swoop overhead. I open my window to see if Rocky Mountain air smells any different than Pennsylvania air.

Once we pass the lakes, the road really begins to climb. The evergreens give way to aspen and birch. We see occasional cars and motorcycles coming and going, but mostly we're alone in the mountains. We must be miles above sea level now, but peaks and summits still tower above us.

The road brings us to a flat, boulder-strewn plain cut by a pretty creek that drops off a nearby hillside. Suddenly, Abbey slams on the brakes. Somehow, neither Kermit nor I am thrown through the windshield. "What was that for?" I yell.

Abbey cuts the steering wheel all the way to the left and takes us through a turn so sharp that we'd have to spin on our heels even if we were walking it. "I was going way too fast," she tells me.

"Then slow down!"

"Thanks for the advice," she mutters.

That first sharp curve leads to several more hairpins that leave both Abbey and me breathless. We're really climbing now, and the roadside is replaced by sheer, boulder-strewn cliffs. A battered guardrail plus an occasional knee-high stone wall are all that stand between us and a thousand-foot drop. "Seriously," I say. "Go slow."

"Seriously," says Abbey, who's got the steering wheel in a white-knuckle grip, "shut up."

Finally, the road flattens out again. We pull into a paved parking area and stop beside a woman who's leaning on a bike. According to a nearby sign, we are sitting atop the Continental Divide, elevation 12,095 feet. There are no other cars around.

"How did you get up here?" Abbey asks the bicyclist when we step out of the Buick.

The woman looks a little older than my mother. "How do you think?"

"You rode a bike up a mountain?" I ask.

"I didn't fly." She looks at our car, then does a double take at the backseat. "Is that what I think it is?"

"What do you think it is?" Abbey asks.

"A dead golden retriever."

"It's what you think it is."

The woman leans toward our back window. "I see shovels back there too."

"So?" says Abbey.

"You can't bury your dog up here."

"Why not?"

"The Rockies are home to several delicate eco-systems. Right now, we're surrounded by alpine tundra and slope meadows that haven't recovered from stage-coach road construction that happened over a hundred years ago. If you bury your dog here, you kill the mountains a little. Is that what you want?"

"Are you some kind of scientist?" I ask.

"I'm a bartender from Aspen who loves this place enough to know a little bit about it."

Abbey puts her hands on her hips. "I just want to bury my dog in a nice spot, okay?"

"You're not going to find any place nicer than this," the woman tells us, "but why do you have to bury him?"

"What do you mean?" asks Abbey.

"Head down the mountain a little. Park on the side of the road, then carry your dog into the woods and leave him someplace out of the way. This whole mountain range can be his tombstone, and you don't need to destroy a single thing."

"Just leave him on the ground?" I say.

"What if something eats him?" Abbey asks.

The woman takes a swig from a water bottle, then snaps her helmet strap beneath her chin. "If you bury him, he'll get eaten by worms and bacteria. Leave him under a tree, and it will be vultures and coyotes. What's the difference? Nature takes us all back one way or another."

"That's reassuring," says Abbey.

"I'm not here to reassure you. I'm here to tell you to do the right thing."

"You rode your bicycle up a mountain so you could tell us to do the right thing?"

"I didn't know it when I started, but apparently that's what the universe had in mind for me today." The woman swings a leg over her bike, turns toward Leadville, and pedals away.

"It would be easier than digging," I suggest after a moment.

"What are we going to do with the shovels?" Abbey asks.

"We're headed toward a dinosaur quarry," I remind her. "They might still come in handy."

Abbey stomps her feet. Even though it's August, it's really cold up here. There are even a few patches of snow nearby. Without warning, my cousin turns and walks away. She slows, then comes to a stop after about twenty yards of pacing. After a moment, she returns. "Okay," she says to me. "I've thought about it. We will lay him on the ground beneath a tree, and the mountains will be his tombstone."

"You're sure?" I say.

"I'm sure that this is the best that we can do." She pauses, then adds "Our best will be good enough for Kermit."

Abbey marches back to the car. I follow, and a moment later, we're back on the road.

The twists and turns make the downhill ride just as scary as coming up. Still, the western side of the Continental Divide is no less beautiful than the east, and the road eventually evens out. When we see a wide patch of gravel, Abbey pulls to the side. Once we're sure no cars are approaching, we work together to wrap Kermit in a blanket. Between us, we carry him away from the Buick and into the woods. There's no trail here, so we have to step carefully over boulders and fallen logs. After a few minutes, we find a dim-lit glade surrounded by evergreens. It's covered in pine needles and sits in the shadow of a mountain peak that rises just above the treetops. The sound of running water comes from somewhere nearby. Without speaking, Abbey and I lay Kermit on the ground. I don't know what mixture of chemistry and spirit and magic and electricity combines to make life, but whatever it is, Kermit doesn't have it anymore.

Chapter Thirteen

We All Look Like Chickens to God

THE ROAD ONLY GOES ONE WAY now, and we ride on it for a long time in sad silence. We pass Aspen and Basalt and Carbondale with the windows wide open and the wind in our faces. Abbey blasts classical music through the car stereo for a while. She says she likes it, but I think it's the only radio station she can find. Eventually the symphony orchestra turns to static, and we follow a winding stream that seems to be home to nothing but fly fishermen and blue herons. Finally, a sign points us back toward the westbound interstate.

Once we're on the highway again, Abbey finds her

phone, then hands it toward me. "Call your mother, and tell her that we'll be in Price, Utah, tonight."

I hold up a Colorado travel guide that I've been reading to pass the time. "I think we should stop in Fruita," I say. "It's home to Mike the Headless Chicken."

"We are not stopping for a headless chicken," Abbey informs me.

I read aloud from the guidebook. "'On September 10, 1945, a strapping but tender young rooster unsuspectingly pecked his way through the dust of Fruita, Colorado. On that now-famous day, Clara Olsen sent her husband, Lloyd, outside with an ax. Lloyd selected the family supper. He grabbed the rooster. He struck. The rooster lost his head'"—I turn to Abbey—"'but the rooster did not die.'"

"That can't be true," says Abbey.

"You're the one who told me that nothing's ever dead and gone," I remind her.

"That doesn't include headless chickens."

I turn back to the guidebook. "'They named the rooster Mike. They fed him with an eyedropper, and they showed him at carnivals and sideshows around the nation for over a year. Fruita is now home to the annual Mike the Headless Chicken Festival.'"

Abbey shakes her head. "I'd say it was a miracle, but God does not perform miracles on chickens."

"Maybe we all look like chickens to God."

"Speaking of chickens," says Abbey, "are you going to call your mother or not?"

I punch Mom's number into Abbey's phone. A moment later, I leave a message. "Hi," I say. "It's Leo."

"I think she'll recognize your voice," says Abbey as she steers us toward the desert.

I wave her away and keep talking. "We drove over the Rocky Mountains this morning. We got chased by a bear. Kermit died." I glance at Abbey. "But we're okay."

Abbey keeps her eyes on the road. "I would have left out the part about the bear."

"We're going to Price, Utah," I continue. "We'll call you when we get there."

"Tonight," says Abbey.

"Tonight," I tell Mom.

"I love you," adds Abbey.

"What?"

"I love you," she says again.

I feel my face burn red. "I—" Suddenly, I realize Abbey is telling me to say the words to my mom. "I love you," I announce more loudly than I mean to. Then I hang up.

Abbey nods. "She'll appreciate that."

Outside, the landscape is remarkably different from the mountains we crossed earlier in the day. We're driving through dry land dotted with scrubby pale bushes, low brown grass, and flat baked hills. We pass the WELCOME TO UTAH sign and stop for a quick break at a town called Green River. From there, we hop onto a long, lonely highway that leads to Price. The road cuts through a wide desert vista surrounded by tall cliffs marked by wide bands of green-and-copper-and-purple-tinted sediment. "This is dinosaur country," Abbey tells me.

"Once upon a time, the whole world was dinosaur country."

Abbey gives a little laugh. "That sounds like something I would say."

After everything that's happened to us in the last twenty-four hours, it's really nice to hear my cousin laugh. "You must be rubbing off on me."

"Only if you're lucky."

"I feel pretty lucky." I also feel worried and afraid and a little carsick. But definitely lucky too.

Abbey laughs again. "I'm glad we're in this together, Leo."

A couple hours later, we pull into the parking lot of the Dinosaur Star Motel on the outskirts of Price, Utah. We step into the lobby, where we find a man-size plastic dinosaur holding a WELCOME sign in one claw and a tray of plastic donuts in the other. Abbey points at the donut-saur. "I think that's a camptosaur. Mr. Kruller should get one for the shop."

A woman standing at the check-in desk turns toward us. "I hear Mr. Kruller is hiring."

"Mom!" I yell.

A second person steps out from behind the dinosaur. "You really think this is a camptosaur?" she asks. "It looks like *Corythosaurus* to me."

"Honey!" shouts Abbey.

Before I know what's happening, Honey and Abbey are hugging and laughing. Mom's crying and kissing my face. The four of us all begin talking at once. The hotel clerk, a skinny blond man standing behind the desk, tries to get our attention. "Are you all together?" he asks.

We ignore him for a moment, so he raises his voice. "I can put your rooms next to one another if you're all together."

"We're all together," Mom tells him.

"Is anybody else joining you?" he asks.

I glance around the lobby. I don't see my grandmother. I look to Mom, who shakes her head. "Gram's not here," she tells me.

"Is anybody else joining you?" the motel guy asks us again. I guess persistence is an important skill in the hotel/motel business.

"We don't know," I tell him.

"It's just us," Mom adds. "For now."

Chapter Fourteen

Joining the Right Circus

AFTER THE HUGS and the tears, we check in at the Dinosaur Star Motel. The four of us pile into a cramped room, where Abbey and I talk about avoiding tow trucks and meeting bears and finally laying Kermit to rest. Mom sits on the lumpy motel bed and leans against a battered wooden headboard. "Unbelievable," she mutters. "Totally unbelievable."

"I know," I say, "but it's all true."

Honey, who's seated on the floor with Abbey, takes my cousin's hand. "Is there anything I can do?"

Abbey shoots me a quick look as if to say, *See? That's how you do it.*

I glance between Honey and Mom. "How did you find each other?" I ask them.

"Your grandmother called my house," says Honey. "Unfortunately nobody was home, so she left a message for Abbey and you."

"What's the message?" I ask.

"She wants you to know that she hasn't lost her mind, that she's making the rest of the trip on her own to prove that she can do it, and that she wants you to stay with my family in Nebraska till she gets back."

"That was never going to happen," Abbey says.

Honey nods. "You'd already left by the time she called."

"Is that why you came to Utah?" I ask. "To deliver Gram's message?"

"Honestly," says Honey, "my parents and I started worrying before you were out of the driveway."

Abbey nudges Honey with her shoulder. "Admit it," she says. "You missed me."

"I didn't like the thought of you wandering around the desert."

"Because you missed me."

"It can be dangerous out there," Honey insists. "I thought you could use a guide."

Abbey makes a face at her.

Honey laughs. "And I missed you."

"But how did you get here before us?" I ask.

Honey stretches her arms out like tattooed wings. "I flew."

"Like Superman?"

"Like Supergirl," says Honey, "if Supergirl had her pilot's license, mountain flight training, and belonged to a flying club that gave her access to small aircraft."

I sit up on the bed. "Wait a minute. You can really fly?"

"I've been flying with my dad since I was twelve. I've had my pilot's license since I was seventeen. There's a lot of empty space in Nebraska, so it's not that unusual around here."

"It might not be unusual to you," says Mom, "but we're impressed."

Abbey turns to Honey. "You're a paleontologist. You've got awesome tattoos. You love your parents. Your parents love you. You've got great hair, and you can fly. Is there any reason why I should not hate you?"

"Don't forget the dead animals in the dishwasher," I say.

"They were already dead!" says Honey.

"Don't hate her because she's beautiful," says Mom. "But the dishwasher thing is a little weird."

I shake my head. "I still don't understand how you found each other."

"Mr. Kruller," Honey explains.

"Mr. Kruller?"

Honey nods. "You told me that Mr. Kruller made the best donuts in Allentown. You also told me he was Abbey's boss, so I tracked him down and gave him a call."

"You really were worried about us."

"So was Mr. Kruller," says Honey. "He put me in touch with your mom."

"Honey phoned me right after I hung up with you," says Mom. "It didn't take long to make a plan from there."

Abbey shoots me a look. "Good thing you called home when you did, huh, Leo?"

I can't even imagine what kind of thermonuclear explosion would have occurred if Mom had learned about Gram's getaway as a result of a phone call from a stranger rather than from me. "Thanks," I whisper to my cousin.

"*De nada,*" she replies.

"Once I landed in Salt Lake City," Mom continues, "all I had to do was rent a car, head for Price, and find the tattooed girl."

"Has anybody talked to Francine?" Abbey asks.

Honey and Mom both shake their heads.

"I tried to call," Mom says. "She doesn't answer."

"She doesn't want to talk to you," I tell my mother.

Mom crosses her arms. "Thanks for saying so, Leo."

"I mean she doesn't want to talk to any of us."

"How do you know that?"

"Leaving us in Nebraska was sort of a clue. Nothing against Nebraska," I add, "but we didn't deserve to be left behind like that."

"I know how you feel," says Mom.

"It doesn't feel good."

"I know." Mom says it a little more firmly this time.

"Oh," I say. "Right." All the family Mom has in the world jumped in a car a few days ago, and then we drove away without her. We didn't even leave a note.

I glance at my mother, who is staring at me. I assume that she's waiting for an apology, but honestly, I am not ready to apologize. I'm always the one who has to apologize. Also, I haven't done anything that I'm particularly sorry about. "I told you it would take a while," I remind my mother.

A tense hush fills the room until Abbey interrupts the silence. "Is anybody hungry?"

"I'm starving," Honey says quickly.

"There's still some Teriyaki-Style Crispy Pusit in the Buick," I offer.

Honey's eyes go wide. "You didn't actually eat that stuff, did you?"

A few minutes later, we squeeze into a booth at a local taqueria. While we study the menu, Mom dips chips into a big bowl of thick red salsa. "That's a dip," I tell her. "Not a soup."

"This might be the best salsa I've ever tasted," she tells me. "Not only that, my mood is improving with every bite. I think you want me to keep eating it, Leo."

"Waiter!" I call out. "More salsa!"

Mom wads up a napkin and throws it at me. "If I knew that traveling would make you so funny, I would have encouraged you to run away and join the circus a long time ago."

"I was just waiting for the right circus to come along," I tell her.

"I don't know if this is the right circus," says Honey, "but it's a pretty good one."

"That's the key to happiness," Abbey declares. "Join the right circus." Mom rolls her eyes.

Dinner arrives quickly. While we dig into huge plates of Mexican food, Mom, Abbey, and Honey all keep their phones on the table, waiting and hoping for them to go off like little time bombs. But Gram never calls. "How about we make a plan for tomorrow?" Abbey finally suggests.

"Do you think Gram might be at the dinosaur quarry already?" I ask.

Abbey shrugs. "It's possible. She could be there right now."

"I've checked out the quarry on a map," Mom informs us. "There is no way we're driving out there tonight. We'll go in the morning."

I'm glad my mother is here. I really am. But we've traveled two thousand miles without her, and I don't appreciate her need to take charge now. Before I can say so, Abbey speaks up. "Honey, what do you think?"

Honey glances outside. The last rays of afternoon sunshine are fading toward night. "By now," she tells us, "the quarry's closed for the day. Francine could be at a campsite, but she could just as easily be at a hotel around the corner. I know the campsites in this area, so we can probably find her if she's out there." Honey turns to me. "The odds of finding her tonight are the same whether we head into the desert now or in the morning. We might as well do what we want and then hope for the best. Do you have a preference, Leo?"

"We'll go in the morning," says Mom.

"Your name is not Leo," I point out.

"We don't need to waste time over this question," Mom says matter-of-factly. "Tomorrow makes better sense."

"You're not in charge of this trip," I tell my mother.

"But I am in charge of you," she replies.

"That doesn't mean you can't let me answer a simple question." I feel my voice start to rise. "You don't have to be so bossy about everything."

"You think I'm bossy?" Mom asks.

Abbey clears her throat. "Excuse me."

"What?" Mom and I both say at the same time.

Abbey puts a hand on my arm, then leans toward my mother. "Auntie Julie," she says in a low voice, "you are a little bossy."

Outside, bright flashes from heat lightning illuminate the evening sky. A tall streetlamp flickers to life above the sidewalk in front of our restaurant, and a long-tailed lizard scampers up the wall behind my mother's head. This conversation would be over in a heartbeat if Mom knew there was a reptile just a few inches away from her neck.

Mom takes a deep breath. "Okay," she finally says.

"Okay, what?" I ask.

"I'm bossy."

I don't say anything because, honestly, I'm sort of stunned.

"So what do you suggest?" she says to me.

"About your bossiness?"

"About when we should go to the dinosaur quarry."

"We should go to the dinosaur quarry in the morning."

My mother's eyes narrow, but she does not speak.

"Just because you're bossy," I tell her, "doesn't mean you're wrong."

Chapter Fifteen

Big Bird's Evil Zombie Cousin and Other Desert Wildlife

MOM, ABBEY, HONEY, and I pile into the Buick early the next morning. On the way out of town, we stop for gas, plus extra snacks and water bottles. "Did you really eat the Crispy Pusit?" Honey asks me while Abbey is pumping gas.

Mom raises an eyebrow.

"It's sort of like beef jerky made out of squid," I explain.

"Squid jerky?" Mom sounds disgusted, but squid jerky is not what's putting the tone in her voice. She's still mad, which I guess is understandable. Abbey, Gram, and I really did abandon her in Allentown. But thinking about the secrets she's kept about my father and Uncle Peter and who knows what else, I'm not too happy with her either.

"I didn't eat the Crispy Pusit," I tell Honey, "but I liked Captain Sid's Butong Pakwan."

Honey, who's wearing a loose T-shirt that says DO YOU DIG? under the picture of a dinosaur skull, laughs. "Maybe you're a little bit Filipino, Leo."

I turn to Mom. "Was my dad from the Philippines?"

Mom considers the question, then opens a box of mini chocolate donuts that we bought at the store. "Your dad was a great big Lithuanian kid from Shenandoah."

I'm stunned into silence for a moment. That's news to me.

"Shenandoah is northwest of Allentown," she adds.

"You never mentioned that before."

Mom pops a mini donut into her mouth. "You never asked."

Abbey finishes with the gas, and we get on our way again. Even though it's August and we're driving through the desert, I'm sitting on my hands and stamping my feet to keep warm. "Can we turn on the heat?" I ask.

Abbey clicks the heater to high.

"Thanks," I tell my cousin.

The car warms up quickly while we head down a two-lane highway leading away from Price. Suddenly, Abbey swerves to avoid a big, bossy-looking bird standing atop a dead thing in the middle of the road. The bird is black and white with a long ebony tail. Even as we roar past, the creature stands its ground. "What was that?" I ask.

Abbey glances in the rearview mirror. "It's either a Utah penguin vulture or Big Bird's evil zombie cousin."

"It's a magpie," says Honey, who's in the backseat with Mom. "You don't have magpies where you live?"

Abbey brings the Buick back to the center of the lane. "Pennsylvania birds get out of the way when they see a car coming."

"Magpies are loud, smart, and stubborn," Honey tells us. "They are not afraid of anything."

Abbey glances between Mom and me. "Who knew we had family in Utah?"

"Very funny," I say.

"If I hadn't swerved," Abbey says, "that magpie could have been cousins with Mike the Headless Chicken."

Honey leans forward from the backseat. "Mike the

Headless Chicken is the weirdest story I ever heard. Did you stop in Fruita?"

"Honey," asks Abbey, "do you just know something about everything?"

Honey points at the dinosaur skull on her shirt. "When you try to learn everything about something, you end up learning something about everything."

A moment later, a roadside sign shaped like a giant brown stegosaur announces, DINOSAURS, TURN AHEAD.

"That sign needs some serious punctuation repair," Abbey observes.

"Are we almost there?" I ask.

Honey shakes her head. "Definitely not."

Abbey cuts the wheel. We veer onto a small, rough road, which leads to a drab intersection anchored by a white steepled church, a low brick post office, and several white and yellow prefab houses. "Welcome to the town of Elmo," proclaims Honey. After about two blocks, she announces, "We are now leaving the town of Elmo."

"Elmo loves you!" says Abbey. "But just for a minute."

Now there is nothing but desert in front of us. "Are you sure we're going the right way?" Mom asks.

"I'm sure," says Honey at about the same time the pavement runs out and the road turns to gravel.

"You're really sure?"

"She said she's sure," I tell my mother.

Honey pulls her hair back into a long ponytail. "As long as we don't miss the next turn, we'll be fine."

"What happens if we miss the next turn?" says Mom.

"We have plenty of food and water," Honey assures her.

"When the food and water run out," says Abbey, "I vote that we should eat Leo first."

"You've got more meat on your bones than I do," I tell my cousin.

Abbey reaches across the front seat and smacks me. "That wasn't nice."

"It's not an insult. It's just a fact."

"Not." *Smack!* "Nice." *Smack!*

"But it's okay to turn me into barbecue?" I ask.

"I think you'd be better as a stew."

"You'd be better as—"

Abbey accidentally steers the Buick through a huge rut in the road. We bounce so hard that I accidentally bite my tongue.

"Ouch!" I yell.

"The two of you!" yells Mom. "Knock it off!"

"Now she's mad at you too," I whisper to my cousin. Unfortunately, I'm not a very good whisperer after a tongue injury.

"So what if I am?" asks Mom.

I turn and face my mother. "You realize that you're the reason we're out here, right?"

"Me?" says Mom.

"You're the one who told me to go after Gram in the first place."

"I told you to bring her home," says Mom. "You brought her to Utah!"

"Technically, he only got her as far as Nebraska," Abbey points out.

"I was doing my best."

"Your best wasn't good enough," says Mom.

"Is that why you're so mad at me?"

"I'm not mad!" The car hits another big bump in the road. "Watch where you're going!" Mom yells at Abbey.

"I'm sure glad you're not mad," Abbey says to Mom.

Mom turns and stares out the window for a moment. "Okay," she says. "Maybe I'm a little mad."

"Why?" Honey asks Mom gently.

Mom takes a deep breath. "My father died a year ago. My mother ran away from home. My son's been wandering around under a black cloud for months." She leans forward and smacks Abbey in the back of the head.

"Hey!" Abbey protests.

"And I love this one like a daughter, which means I worry about her all the time."

Abbey glances at the rearview mirror and gives Mom a little smile. "I love you too, Auntie Julie."

"I'm trying to keep a lot of balls in the air," Mom says. "It feels like I'm doing it all by myself, and you know what?"

"What?" says Honey.

"It's really hard."

Honey nods. "Maybe you should drop a few."

Mom turns to Honey. "That's not the kind of advice I'd expect from Supergirl."

"In real life," Honey tells Mom, "there's no such thing as Supergirl."

Mom doesn't reply.

"It's like Leo says," Honey adds.

I glance between Honey and Mom. "What do I say?" I ask.

Honey turns in her seat to face me and my mother. "We are all just doing our best."

Mom looks like she's about to reply. Before she can speak, however, Abbey slams on the brakes. "Hey!" Mom shouts as a cloud of dust explodes around the Buick.

"What was that for?" I ask when we finally skid to a stop.

Abbey points at the road ahead of us. "SNAKE!"

At first, I see nothing. When the dust settles, however, a golden-brown snake with diamond-patterned skin lies almost all the way across the road. It's longer than the Buick is wide with a body that's at least as thick as my arm. In other words, it's a very big snake.

"Whoa," I say.

Honey opens her door, grabs an old umbrella from beneath the seat, then takes a few tentative steps forward. Abbey hops out of the car and follows. "I'll be right back," I tell Mom.

Mom shakes her head. "I'll stay right here." She does not like snakes.

Outside, Honey reaches out with the umbrella and gives the snake a gentle prod.

"What are you doing?" I ask.

"We have to make her move," Honey whispers. "Otherwise, she could get run over by a car." She gives the snake another nudge. Several feet away, its tail gives a little twitch.

"Don't make it mad!" I say.

"She's probably too cold to get mad," Honey tells me. "That's why she's lying in the sun."

I remember that snakes are cold-blooded. When the temperature drops, they can get slow and groggy. "Be careful," I say.

"Don't worry," says Honey, "she's just a big—"

Suddenly, the snake gives off a sharp *hiss-hiss-hiss*, then wraps itself into a coil. It quickly turns to face Honey, then begins shaking its tail like a—

"RATTLESNAKE!" I scream. "GET BACK!" I'm torn between jumping onto the roof of the car and rushing forward to pull Honey to safety. I decide that I'd rather die a hero. I sprint to Honey's side, grab her wrist, and begin to drag her away.

"Leo!" she says.

"I'VE GOT YOU!" I tell her.

"Leo!" she says again. This time, I can't help noticing that Honey is laughing.

"What?"

Honey uses her free hand to point at the road. "You scared her away."

Sure enough, the snake is racing off the road and into the desert as quickly as possible. I stop and stare at the retreating reptile. "And stay away!" I yell after it.

"That was a bull snake," Honey tells me. "They're not dangerous."

"Didn't you see it coil up and shake its tail?" I tell her. "That was a rattlesnake!"

"Bull snakes pretend to be rattlesnakes. That's how they scare away predators. Pretty convincing, huh?"

A few yards away, the snake is still speeding through the scrub brush. "I was convinced," I admit.

Honey turns to me after the snake disappears from view. "You really thought it was a rattlesnake?"

I nod.

"And you came to save me?"

"I almost ran away," I confess.

"But you didn't."

"I guess not."

"Thank you."

"For saving you from nothing?" I ask.

"It wasn't nothing to you," says Honey, "so it's not nothing to me."

Abbey steps forward and punches me in the shoulder. "How does it feel to be a hero, Leo?"

"It feels like I'm going to throw up," I admit.

My cousin gives me a big grin. "They never talk about that part in the comic books, huh?"

Chapter Sixteen

Styrofoamosaurus

THE DESERT ROAD winds and turns for several more miles, then finally brings us to a tall metal gate covered in peeling yellow paint and big patches of rust. "We're here," Honey announces.

Around us, there's nothing but huge blue sky, gigantic stacks of golden-brown rocks, and an endless vista of rolling desert. "I don't see any dinosaurs," says Abbey.

"I don't see any grandmothers," says Mom.

"Keep driving," says Honey.

We go through the gate and follow the road for another hundred yards until we top a small rise. Below, a small building made of stone and wood stands alone in the desert. Honey points at the structure. "That's the visitor center. There's a walking trail in back that leads to the dig site."

Abbey steers the Buick into a gravel parking lot and shuts off the engine. We all step out of the car and walk to the visitor center entrance, where a long wooden sign says, CLEVELAND-LLOYD DINOSAUR QUARRY. Abbey presses her face against a big window near the front door. "I see a dinosaur!" she hollers.

"I still don't see any grandmothers," says Mom.

As a matter of fact, we don't see anybody at all. Other than a small white pickup truck parked nearby, we have the entire desert to ourselves. Abbey grabs the visitor center door handle and pulls it open. "I'm going in!" she announces.

Honey, Mom, and I follow close behind. A couple green-and-gray lizards race out of our way, while a small bird with a bright yellow chest scolds us from beneath an overhang. "That's a kingbird," says Honey.

"Where's the queen?" asks Mom.

Honey opens the visitor center door and points inside. "Come and see for yourself."

Inside, Honey directs us toward a mounted allosaur that's standing in the middle of the room. Even though it's just a skeleton, the animal is awesome. And for some reason—maybe it's the allosaur's posture or strength or grace—it's clear that Honey is right. This creature is regal. She's twenty-five feet long and a dozen feet high. She leans forward into a sprint with her tail raised high like a gun dog on the hunt. Her head tilts to the side as if she's just caught sight of her prey.

Abbey steps to the railing that circles the display. She stares straight into the allosaur's open mouth. "Imagine what it was like when this thing had eyes and skin and breath."

"I bet it had really bad breath," I say.

Abbey studies the dagger-shaped teeth mounted inside the allosaur skull. "You probably wouldn't have to smell its breath for very long."

Mom glances around. "Does anybody work here?"

"They're down at the quarry," says Honey.

"How do you know?" I ask

Honey points to a handwritten sign taped onto the railing. It says, WELCOME. I'M AT QUARRY. BE RIGHT BACK.—RANGER REYNALDO.

"Let's go see what Ranger Reynaldo is up to," says Mom.

We head back outside and follow a paved sidewalk toward a long metal hut that sits at the base of a rocky hill. The cooler morning air has been cooked off by the sun, and now it's turning dry and hot. It's even warmer inside the hut, where we find the ranger standing in the middle of a huge collection of black dinosaur bones strewn around a deep, wide hole in the floor.

"That's a lot of bones," says Abbey.

At the sound of Abbey's voice, Ranger Reynaldo looks up. He's a balding, round-faced man in loose-fitting pants, high-top hiking boots, and a short-sleeved, collared shirt. The pants, shoes, and shirt are all the same sandy brown color as his tan face and arms. With all that brown, he could lie down on the desert floor and blend right in. "Hello there," he calls from among the bones. "I'm just doing a little housekeeping." The ranger reaches toward a huge black fossil that's roughly the size of a dump-truck tire.

"Is that a pelvis?" Abbey asks.

"It is," says Ranger Reynaldo.

"But it's not an allosaur pelvis," says Honey.

"You're right," says the ranger. "It's from a stegosaur. I'm impressed."

"How did you know?" I ask Honey.

"Leo," Abbey says to me, "allosaur pelvises and stegosaur pelvises are completely different."

"Exactly," says Honey.

"Obviously," says Abbey.

The two girls laugh. It strikes me that we've only known Honey for about three days, but I think Abbey and Honey are going to be friends for life.

The ranger reaches forward, grabs the stegosaur fossil, and lifts it over his head with one arm. With his free hand, he retrieves an empty potato chip bag that was stuck in the dirt beneath the bone.

"That's not possible," says Abbey.

The ranger lowers the fossil, then holds up the trash. "With human beings anything is possible."

Abbey points at the big pelvis. "I mean you can't lift that. Fossils are rocks. That pelvis must weigh a couple hundred pounds."

"It's actually a lot heavier than that. It's also worth over half a million dollars. That's why we don't keep the real one in a metal garden shed protected by a hardware store lock in the middle of the desert." Ranger Reynaldo nudges the stegosaur pelvis with his toe. "This is a reproduction made out of Styrofoam and black spray paint." He points at the bones spread around us. "Most of this stuff is Styrofoam. The real fossils are too valuable to leave lying around."

Somehow, this fact makes me feel happy and sad at the exact same time. I'm happy because this dinosaur quarry is for real and not some kind of prehistoric theme park. But honestly, we drove a long, long way just to see Styrofoam. We could have probably stayed home for that.

"Don't worry," says Ranger Reynaldo, who must have noticed the disappointment in my face. "It's not all Styrofoam." He reaches down and retrieves a fossil from the ground. You can tell from the way he lifts the thing that it must be heavy. "Hold out your hand," he instructs me.

I do as I'm told, and the ranger places a long, smooth stone that's shaped like a fat, pointy spike into my palm. "Allosaur tooth?" I guess.

"*Camptosaurus* toe," he tells me.

I feel the weight of the fossil in my hand. It is millions of years old, and it's definitely not Styrofoam. "This is amazing."

"I'm glad you think so."

"Speaking of fossils," says Mom, "did you happen to see an old lady around here lately?"

"Did you lose an old lady?" Ranger Reynaldo asks.

"Sort of," Abbey tells him.

"I might be able to help with that." He takes the camptosaur toe back from me, climbs out of the hole, and then leads us outside, where the temperature feels like it's gone up another twenty or thirty degrees. "An elderly woman driving a Jeep with Nebraska plates passed through Elmo this morning."

"That's her!" I say.

"She stopped at the Elmo post office and asked the clerk there for directions to the dinosaur quarry."

"How do you know what she said to the clerk?" I ask.

"I live in Elmo. It's a very small town, and I happen to be married to the postal clerk. She radioed and let me know to expect company. But you're the only visitors I've had today."

"Radioed?" says Mom.

"Cell phones aren't that dependable out here."

I stare at the rough wilderness that stretches for miles and miles around us. Back in Pennsylvania, we have mountains and rivers and forests, but I never imagined visiting a huge, untamed place like this. In my mind, this kind of wilderness existed only far, far away in Africa or in the rain forest or in *National Geographic*. I didn't know we had it right here in the United States of America.

"She must have missed the turn," the ranger tells us now. "Hopefully she'll backtrack, but most people take the next left by mistake."

"Where does that go?" I ask.

"It dead-ends at a picnic area on top of a high ridge. There's no water there, but it's a million-dollar view."

"We've got water," I say.

"What if she missed that second left?" asks Mom.

Ranger Reynaldo adjusts his hat, which looks just like the one Smokey Bear wears. "Then she's going to have a long, cold night in the desert."

Chapter Seventeen

How to Avoid Extinction

I HOPE THERE ARE NO SNAKES in the road because Mom is driving now and we are flying across the desert like a rocket-powered bulldozer attached to a heat-seeking missile. "Hey!" Abbey yells. "Slow down!"

"Did you hear Ranger Reynaldo?" says Mom. "If we don't find my mother, she'll have to sleep in the desert!"

Abbey leans forward from the backseat, where she's sitting with Honey. "We're not going to find her if you kill us first."

The Buick hits a deep rut, and we bounce around the car like Ping-Pong balls inside a tin can. "This is a pre-airbag vehicle," I remind my mother.

Mom lets up on the gas, but only a little. We hit another pothole. This time, the glove compartment pops open and a pile of pens and papers drops into my lap. "Slow down!" Abbey yells again.

Mom lets our speed drop to the point where a sonic boom is unlikely. I try to stuff everything back into the glove box, but I can't make it fit. Meanwhile, Mom fish-tails around corners and skips across the washboard road. Her driving is making me feel sick, so I lower my window and stick my head outside. It feels a bit like leaning into a blast furnace, but the dry air helps my stomach a little.

Mom grabs my shirt and yanks me back into my seat. "What do you think you're doing?"

"I'm trying not to vomit."

"Push him back outside!" Abbey shouts.

Honey hands me a water bottle from the back. "Take small sips."

Following Ranger Reynaldo's instructions, we turn at a sign for CEDAR MOUNTAIN RECREATION AREA. The road begins to rise, but Mom does not slow down. Outside, tough-looking trees with weird, twisty trunks interrupt the vista. The desert vegetation here shows a slightly darker shade of green than the low cactus and dry brush that surrounded the dinosaur quarry. "What are those trees?" I ask Honey.

"Pinyon pines and cedars. They can live five or six hundred years." Honey points at one of the cedars. "That tree was probably here before Benjamin Franklin started flying kites in thunderstorms."

Mom shakes her head. "My father and I tried to re-create that experiment for my middle school science fair."

This is scary, shocking, and totally believable. "What happened?" I ask.

Mom shrugs. "We survived."

I wonder how many stories, both big and small, are still left for me to discover about my family.

Our car hits another big bump, and we bounce off the seats. In the back, Abbey rubs the top of her head, which just knocked into the roof. "I'd like to survive," she says.

"If you wanted to avoid extinction," says Mom, "then you should have stayed home."

"Actually," says Honey, "that won't work either."

"Then how do you avoid extinction?" I ask.

"Eventually," Honey tells me, "you don't."

"You do realize," Abbey tells Honey, "that in this car, you're the optimistic one."

Honey shrugs. "I have a professor who says that humans only remember each other for about three generations. He says it's our nature to leave our great-grandparents and our great-great-grandparents and everybody that came before them behind."

"I'm not leaving anybody behind," I say.

"Leo," says Abbey, "you don't even know your father's name."

"Thanks," I tell my cousin.

"Walter," says Mom as she swerves around a depression in the road.

"Walter?" I say.

Mom nods.

"Walter the Lithuanian volleyball player from Shenandoah." Abbey reaches over the backseat and gives my shoulder a squeeze. "Slowly but surely, we are assembling a picture of this mystery man, Leo."

Mom glances at my cousin in the rearview mirror. "How did you know about the volleyball?"

Before Abbey can reply, Honey points at a sudden

bright reflection shimmering in the distance. "Is that a car?" she asks.

Neither Abbey, Mom, nor I can make out any details in the distance. I reach into my backpack, find Pop's binoculars, and bring them to my face. "It's a Jeep!" I yell.

Mom pushes the accelerator to the floor.

The road continues to climb while the landscape drops away to our right. We're on top of a wide, flat plateau. Below us, tall brown ridges rise like gigantic waves out of the desert floor. A tiny white dot glides through the sky in front of the nearest ridge. At first, I assume that the dot is some kind of pale desert bird, but when I look through the binoculars, I see that it's a white jet plane streaking across the western U.S. The scale of the land changes so fast in my head that it almost makes me dizzy.

Abbey reaches over my shoulder and grabs the binoculars. "Let me see those."

"They're around my neck."

Abbey ignores my protests and pulls the binoculars to her face. The leather strap tightens around my throat.

"I can't breathe!" I gasp.

"That's definitely Francine's Jeep," Abbey announces. "It's parked on the side of the road." She drops the binoculars and pats me on the back. "You can inhale now, Leo."

I take a big gulp of air. "Thanks a lot."

A moment later, we skid to a stop behind the dusty green Jeep. We step out of the Buick and into desert air that smells like beach sand and popcorn and dried-out Christmas trees.

"Francine?" Abbey yells.

"Mom?" calls Mom.

Honey jogs to the front of the Jeep. "Over here!" she shouts.

We catch up with Honey and find Gram just a few yards away. She's wearing a straw cowboy hat, her high-tops, and a loose cotton work shirt over a pair of baggy green gardening pants. She's sitting on a folding lawn chair and staring over the edge of the cliff at the desert floor several thousand feet below.

"Gram?" I say.

"It took you long enough to find me," she replies.

"How long have you been here?"

Gram kicks a stone off the cliff. "About an hour."

"We left Nebraska City about an hour after you did."

Gram considers this. "I suppose that means you're right on time." She gets out of her chair, then turns to face me. She points at the binoculars still hanging around my neck. "Your grandfather loved those things."

"They've come in handy," I admit.

Honey steps forward. "Are you okay?" she asks my grandmother.

"Honey Buenafe! Check this out!" Gram rolls up her sleeve and reveals a lively black allosaur tattoo dancing across her forearm.

"Nice!" says Honey.

I admit that I want to yell at her. Instead, I decide that first, Gram is an adult. If she wants a tattoo, then she should have a tattoo. Second, her allosaur tattoo really does look awesome. And third, no tattoo—not even a dancing allosaur—is going to make Gram more or less wonderful to me than she already is. I love her, she's safe, and that's all that matters.

"I got it in Denver," Gram says. "It hurt a lot more than I expected."

Before Honey can reply, Mom steps out from behind the Jeep. "You got a tattoo?"

Gram's head snaps around. "What are you doing here?"

Mom takes a half step back. "It's nice to see you too."

"And?" says Gram.

"And I've come to take you home."

"To *my* home?" Gram asks. "Or to *a* home?"

Mom sighs. "I'm sorry."

Gram puts a hand to her mouth and begins to cough. Abbey runs back to the Buick, then returns a moment later with two bottles of water.

"Here," she says to Gram.

Gram takes a bottle, twists the cap open, removes her cowboy hat, then pours water over her head. "I needed to cool down."

Abbey laughs. "I missed you, old lady."

"That's because you're a smart girl." Gram takes the second water bottle and moves closer to the Jeep. Abbey drags the chair over so that Gram can sit. I lean against the bumper while Honey remains standing. Mom drops down to sit in the sand.

"I wouldn't do that," Honey warns her.

"Why not?" she asks.

"Fire ants, scorpions, rattlesnakes, wolf spiders . . ."

Mom leaps to her feet, then joins me on the bumper. "When did we leave America and enter the wild kingdom?"

I think back to Ohio's starry skies and Chicago's inland sea and our own hometown rivers. I recall snowcapped mountains, a million acres of corn, a giant frightened snake, and an angry bear with her cubs. Not to mention dinosaurs. "Mom," I say, "I think it might all be kind of wild."

That makes Gram laugh.

"We were worried about you," I tell her.

"You should be worried about me." Gram takes a sip from the water. "I've been worried about me."

"You have?"

"Of course!" Gram says. "I'm old. I'm lonely. I'm afraid. I want to do things I can't do anymore. Plus, I got lost in the desert, and I didn't know how to find my way out. Do you want me to go on?"

Mom shakes her head. "Why did you come here?"

Gram looks to Abbey and me.

"This trip was never really about dinosaurs," I say now. "Was it?"

"Probably not," Gram admits.

"Then what's it about?" I ask.

"Maybe it's about figuring out what it's about," says Honey.

Abbey gives a Honey a quick grin. "That was spoken like a true scientist, journalist, novelist, and historian."

I remind my cousin of my own life philosophy. "I haven't figured it out yet."

"Don't worry," Gram tells me. "Nobody else has either."

Chapter Eighteen

A Tragedy with Knock-Knock Jokes

AFTER A LONG TIME, we get back on the desert road. Abbey and Honey ride in the Jeep with Gram, I stay in the Buick with Mom, and we all drive back to the Cleveland-Lloyd Dinosaur Quarry, where Ranger Reynaldo is very happy to see us. Inside the visitor center, I show Gram the mounted allosaur.

Gram studies the skeleton. "This is not really a dinosaur," she says after a while.

"It's definitely a dinosaur," says Abbey, who proceeds to read aloud from an information sheet posted on a nearby wall.

"'*Allosaurus fragilis* was a bipedal, carnivorous dinosaur that lived a hundred and fifty to a hundred and fifty-five million years ago during the Late Jurassic period. An active predator of large animals, allosaurs had an average estimated length of twenty-eight feet and may have weighed up to five thousand pounds.'"

Gram points at the big fossil in the middle of the room. "This is just a pile of rocks in the shape of a dinosaur."

"And we're just fleshy bags of water in the shape of people," says Abbey. "What's your point?"

"The dinosaurs are gone," Gram says. "My husband is gone. My son is gone." She glances at Mom. "Your brother is gone."

Mom doesn't reply.

"'All our yesterdays have lighted fools the way to dusty death,'" Gram says softly.

"Is that Shakespeare?" says Abbey. "I swear that guy has something to say about everything."

"That's from *Macbeth*," says Honey. "And as far as dusty death, that's my career path you're talking about."

That gets a smile from Gram. Mom actually laughs out loud, which is a surprise because this does not necessarily feel like a comic relief moment. "You and Dad took me to see a high school performance of *Macbeth* when I was little," Mom says to Gram. "I know *Macbeth* is a tragedy, but do you know what I remember about it?"

"What?" asks Gram.

"Right in the middle there's a knock-knock joke."

"There is not," Gram says to Mom.

"Look it up," says Mom. "It's a tragedy with knock-knock jokes."

Gram rolls her eyes. "A tragedy with knock-knock jokes. That's the story of my life."

"If it's got knock-knock jokes," says Abbey, "then it must be a comedy."

"Knock knock," says Gram.

Abbey ignores her.

"Knock knock," Gram says again.

"Resistance is futile," I tell my cousin.

"KNOCK KNOCK," Gram repeats loudly.

Abbey relents. "Who's there?"

"Honey Bee," says Gram.

"Honey Bee who?" asks Abbey.

Gram turns to Honey. "Honey, be a dear and tell Abbey the difference between comedy and tragedy."

Honey nods. "In comedies, people get what they need. In tragedies, characters get crushed like bugs so that the audience can feel better about themselves."

I raise my hand. "I vote for comedy."

Chapter Nineteen

The First Story

THE NEXT MORNING, we take Honey to the Price airport. She hugs me, Mom, and Gram, and then she takes my cousin by the hand. "Abbey," she says, "when you are most with you, and I am most with me, then we are most together."

"What does that mean?" Abbey asks.

"I have no idea," Honey admits. "It's something my dad tells me whenever we say good-bye."

"Is it an old Filipino saying?"

Honey shakes her head. "I think he got it out of a comic book, but it's nice, isn't it?"

A few minutes later, Honey's airplane, a bright

red-and-white two-seater that's not much bigger than our Buick, lifts off the runway. She makes a big loop in the sky above us, waggles her wings once, then heads east toward Nebraska. I watch through Pop's binoculars until her plane fades into the blue sky.

Together, Mom, Gram, Abbey, and I turn toward the green Jeep. It's parked beside our Electra, which Abbey drove through a car wash after we got back from the desert. Now the yellow Buick is shiny and clean. It looks as if it could go another ten thousand miles without any problem.

"Who's taking me back to Salt Lake City?" Mom asks. Since we have two cars, Mom already returned her rental.

Neither Gram nor Abbey speaks. I look up at the sapphire sky and the sandstone cliffs in the distance. "What are you going to do with the Jeep?" I ask my grandmother.

"I should probably take it back to Nebraska," she says.

"You paid for it," I remind her. "It's yours."

Abbey clears her throat. "Why not keep going?"

Nobody speaks.

"There's still lots to see," she adds.

Gram offers half a smile. "I wouldn't want to do it alone."

"I'd come," says Abbey, "if you promise not to abandon me somewhere."

Gram's got a big grin now. She turns to me. "What about you, Leo?"

I glance at my mother. She runs a hand through her hair and bites her lower lip. I know she wants to go home. To be honest, so do I.

"I know it's a long way," I say to Mom, "but maybe you and I could drive back to Pennsylvania together."

"Really?" says Mom.

"I'd like that," I tell her.

Mom is quiet for a moment. "I'd like that too," she finally replies.

A few moments later, Gram is behind the wheel of the Jeep. Abbey's in the passenger seat beside her. "Don't forget the Liquid Carb Doctor," my cousin reminds me.

"Don't forget to send a postcard from everywhere you go," I tell her.

"Be careful!" Mom says to both Abbey and Gram.

"Take care of my grandson," Gram replies.

The Jeep begins to roll away, but then I remember one more thing. "Wait!" I shout.

Gram slams on the brakes. The Jeep jerks to a stop. I sprint to Gram's window.

"What is it, Leo?"

I take the binoculars that are still hanging around my neck. I lift them over my head and hand them to my grandmother. "These should go with you."

Gram smiles. "Your grandfather would want you to keep them."

I admit that I'd really like to hold on to the binoculars for myself. Somehow, having them with me during these past few days has made it feel like Pop is nearby. That's been a very good feeling. It's a feeling I'd like Gram to have too. But before my grandmother can accept my offer, Abbey leans across the seat. "Leo," she says to me, "you have to take those with you."

"No," I say.

"Yes," says Abbey. "And then one night soon, you take your mother outside, you hand her those binoculars, and you let her show you the stars. That's what Pop would want."

Sudden tears well up in my grandmother's eyes. "Abbey is a very smart girl," Gram tells me.

I put the binoculars back around my neck. "I'm going to miss you both."

"We are your family." Gram leans forward and kisses me on the head. "We are always with you."

"Like it or not," adds Abbey.

"For better or worse," says Gram.

They pull away, leaving Mom and me standing beside the Buick Electra in the Utah heat. "Leo," says Mom, "you really want to be stuck in a car together for two thousand miles?"

"I do," I say.

"It will definitely give us time to talk." Mom hesitates. "I know you want to hear about your father."

"I want to hear about everything."

Mom doesn't reply, so I keep going.

"I want to hear about my uncle Peter. I want to know about the science experiments you did with Pop when you were little. I want you to tell me everything about Walter the Lithuanian volleyball player. I want to know about you. I want to know about me. I want you to tell me all the stories."

My mother looks shocked at the flood of words that just rushed out of me. Even I'm a little stunned. "Leo," Mom says, "get in the car."

I pull the passenger-side door open and slide onto the front seat while Mom settles behind the steering wheel.

"Your grandmother told you about Peter?"

I nod.

"Listen," she says. "I'm not a jukebox. You can't just put a nickel in me, punch a button, and get a story."

"Jukeboxes only cost a nickel?"

"Once upon a time," Mom says.

"Once upon a time is a good way to begin," I say.

Mom finds the key and fits it into the ignition. "Can I make a suggestion?"

She's going to make her suggestion no matter how I respond, so I say, "Yes."

"How about we start a new story?"

I shake my head. "No."

Mom looks surprised. "No?"

"I think we're already sort of in the middle of a

story," I explain. "Maybe it started back when Gram dreamt about killing Pop and married him instead."

"She told you about that too?"

"It probably starts before then if you think about it."

"I'm sure it goes back to Greek mythology and the big bang theory and 'Let there be light' if you let it, Leo. What's your point?"

"I'm just saying that it's hard to be ready for whatever might come next when I have no idea about all the things that happened first."

Mom sits without speaking for a long time. Finally, she turns to me. "Okay," she says.

"Okay, what?" I ask.

"I will tell you stories."

"All the stories?"

"All the stories."

Now it's my turn to sit without speaking because honestly, I have no idea what I'm in for.

"Leo," Mom says.

"Yeah?"

"Before we start with all the stories, can we figure out where we're going today?"

I nod. That's fair. It's even a little bit of a relief. I think it would be good for us both to have the car rolling, the windows down, and the breeze blasting in our faces before we begin.

I notice the Colorado guidebook on the seat between us, so I open it to a familiar page. "There's a town called Fruita," I tell my mother. "It's a few hours away. It's home to the annual Mike the Headless Chicken Festival."

Mom laughs. She turns the key in the ignition, and the Buick roars to life. "A festival for headless chickens? That sounds like a place we need to see."

Acknowledgments

My heartfelt thanks goes to Nancy Mercado and Susan Hawk, who are joyful and inspiring friends and partners in this storytelling adventure. Thanks also to all the folks at Scholastic whose work brings this and so many other books to life.

David Lubar, Jordan Sonnenblick, Josh Berk, Erin Dionne, Elizabeth Bluemle, and many more are among a group of remarkable and talented writers and friends who all seem to know exactly when I need a kind word, a laugh, or a bit of encouragement. Thank you!

My sincere gratitude to the Enormous, Colossal, Astonishing, Dumbfounding, Terrifying, Extraordinary, Incredible awesomeness of Chicago's Field Museum and the Cleveland-Lloyd Dinosaur Quarry. Places like these, along with the people who manage and share them, are national treasures. Please visit and support them!

Thank you to the generous and remarkable Glendon Mellow, who allowed me to use his allosaur tattoo. If

I ever get a tattoo, I'm going to call Glendon. (Check out Glendon's artwork at glendonmellow.com. You'll be glad you did.)

I am also very grateful to the real-life Abbey Jones and her family for being part of this escapade. Speaking of escapades, everything I do is more exciting, more fun, more rewarding, and more possible because of my own family. Nicholas, Gabrielle, and especially my wife and best friend, Debbie . . . thank you most of all!

About the Author

Paul Acampora has written three previous novels, and people have said nice things about each of them. Kids, parents, and critics praise his work for its laugh-out-loud humor, rollicking dialogue, and heartfelt characters. *School Library Journal* called his debut novel, *Defining Dulcie*, "an inextricable mix of sadness and humor, sorrow and hope." *Kirkus Reviews* said his next novel, *Rachel Spinelli Punched Me in the Face*, was "an outstanding, humane coming-of-age tale of loss, yearning, and forgiveness," and *Booklist* called *I Kill the Mockingbird* a "well-written, resolutely cheerful offering [that] celebrates books, reading, and life." You can find Paul online at www.paulacampora.com.